THE Resolute PRINCE

nana prah

First Published in Great Britain in 2021 by
LOVE AFRICA PRESS
103 Reaver House, 12 East Street, Epsom KT17 1HX
www.loveafricapress.com

LOVE AFRICA
PRESS
African Love Stories

Also available as paperback

ROYAL HOUSE OF SAENE

THE PRINCESSES:
His Defiant Princess by Nana Prah
His Inherited Princess by Empi Baryeh
His Captive Princess by Kiru Taye

THE PRINCES:
The Torn Prince by Zee Monodee
The Resolute Prince by Nana Prah
The Tainted Prince by Kiru Taye
The Illegitimate Prince by Empi Baryeh
The Future King by Kiru Taye

BLURB

As head of palace security Prince Zareb Saene lives to protect the Royal House of Saene. Between his work and coaching competitive fencing, he has no time for relationships. That is, until he meets the beautiful and headstrong Malika Ahvanti. She scales his carefully constructed walls and lands squarely in his heart. If only he could shake this unwarranted, illicit pull towards her younger brother, the new fencing protégé that he's been charged with training.

Malika dreams of becoming an Olympic gold medalist and is determined to succeed. Training with the Lion of Bagumi is her only chance, but after past deceptions, he refuses to coach females. Getting what she wants comes at an uncomfortable price. With great risk she presents herself as a young man with promising skill. The guilt of lying compounded by her undeniable desire for Zareb puts her future in jeopardy and her heart in danger.

CHAPTER ONE

"That's enough!"

Prince Zareb Saene's bellow resounded with a deep frustration disproportional to the actions he'd just witnessed from his fencing trainees.

His students ceased sparring and lowered their swords.

Zareb held out a gloved hand to receive the épée from the shorter of the two young men, Rafi, before waving him aside. The thin, blunted sword was lighter than his own, but he'd make do. Putting on protective gear would be optimal, but he knew for a fact that the trainee lacked the skills to come anywhere close to scoring a point against him.

"The flick is a complicated move. Timing and gauging are critical," he said while adjusting his stance into the basic *en garde* position.

His opponent, Salim, mimicked the stance with his épée, prepared to fight.

"Attack with an advance-lunge."

The young man nodded.

"*Allez!*" Zareb gave the word to begin.

Salim sprang forward and aimed his sword.

With the ease of swatting the air, Zareb stepped backwards while blocking the attack. Gaging the distance, he took the slightest step forward, raised his elbow, and whipped his épée, stopping it at the last moment so that the tip hit his student's shoulder.

"Again."

With the expertise that had won him bronze in the 2016 Summer Olympics, he demonstrated the move two more times at full speed. Then he slowed the pace and explained what they had been doing wrong with the advanced procedure.

Handing the weapon back to Rafi, he clapped him hard on the shoulder. "Now, you try."

He crossed his arms over his chest in an attempt to contain the light buzz of adrenalin humming through his system. Anytime he had an épée in his hand, the strong desire to pounce on his competition emerged. The need to excel at what he set his determined mind to would never be abated. To be the best meant everything.

Rafi slid his mask over his head and stepped onto the *piste*. After several attempts, he shook out his hand and winced.

"Your turn, Salim," Zareb said.

The less experienced of the two did no better.

He kept the disappointment out of his voice. "Practice until you can no longer hold your sword."

That would teach them to skip out on grip-strengthening exercises.

"Yes, Your Highness," they answered in unison, not daring to express a single objection.

Discipline. He demanded it in his training facility and his life.

He lifted his gaze to assess the establishment his father had built for him so he could bring glory to Bagumi. His coaches drilled the other participants who had come to train. Their facility was the largest in Africa, boasting of ten fencing strips. Each piste was electronically enhanced with wireless signals, just as they'd be found in the Olympics.

The 200-metre elevated running track allowed the trainees to gain physical endurance in an air-conditioned environment when the weather grew too stifling to jog outside. After torturing himself by running in the sweltering West African sun for years, Zareb had insisted on the structure.

A state-of-the-art gym and swimming pool sat on the other side of the glass where the security-vetted members could watch the fencers' practice if they were interested.

Assessing the manoeuvres of the twenty men and women who paid to train in his facility, dissatisfaction clutched at his heart. Where was the greatness he was searching for? He had yet to teach anyone with the skill and potential to get anywhere near the Olympics. No matter how many hours they practised or how hard he pushed the ones who came to him, he'd never seen that grit and determination to make winning the only thing that mattered. He hadn't witnessed himself in anyone.

He'd hung up his competitive sword too early. At twenty-eight, he still had a lot of wins left in him. Yet, as fit as he was, he was not in Olympic condition. He could gain it back. Exhaustive hours training with his mind laser-focused on fencing all day every day would probably kill him. But at least, he'd have that renewed sense of accomplishment back.

No one can serve two masters. His initial failure on his climb to the Olympics had taught him that tough lesson. He'd made his choice and had no option but to stick with it.

The hollowness in his chest at losing the chance to be the best at what he loved with a passion he'd never felt for anything else would pass. Even if it didn't, it wouldn't matter—he had chosen the more worthy of the two masters. To protect his family. Nothing else was more important. Not even his own happiness.

A familiar heat pulsed into his back. He turned to find his twin brother Zediah holding his son. Zed dipped his head towards Zareb's office, expecting him to follow.

Zareb retreated from the cling of clashing metal swords and closed the door to his soundproof office, where the silence rang in his ears.

His eighteen-month-old nephew raised his hands and squealed.

Reflex brought out the smile reserved for the toddler he lifted into his arms.

"Hey, Nour." Zareb tugged on a strand of the boy's hair. Nour grabbed a fistful of Zareb's bound locs and pulled as he giggled. At least he'd stopped trying to eat the strands as he'd been prone to do when he'd been teething. Being around the child lightened his mood.

He then focused on his brother. "Where's your guard?"

No one could tell they were twins—not by face, physique, or personality. Zareb was stern and had to have control over every aspect of his and everyone else's life. Zed was more laidback, artistic to the point of being inspiring, and gentle to everyone he encountered. People gravitated to Zed and fled from Zareb. Just the way he liked it.

Zed shook his head. "Don't start."

Not likely. "You're the one who called off the marriage with the president of Barakat's daughter. Tensions are high between our countries. Her father is resisting the settlement of the territorial water disputes that your marriage to Bilkiss would've eradicated."

Zed's eyes narrowed, expression stern. "Guilty as charged. And I'd do it all over again to have Rio and Nour in my life."

Zareb's arm flexed around Nour, who'd decided to pinch his cheek and laugh. He was overprotective of everyone in the royal family, but he would never forgive himself if something happened to his nephew. "General Noda isn't known for his beneficent and forgiving nature. He's a good ally but a formidable foe. Thanks to you, we're on his vengeful side."

The comment was met with Zed's gimlet stare. His brother would make no apologies for putting Bagumi at risk. "Don't forget that it wasn't all me. Bilkiss ran from the impending wedding."

"True, but you are a Saene, not the blood relative of the General. I doubt that he would hesitate to try to make you pay. You have a family to look after now," Zareb grunted with jealousy at his twin's ability to have chosen to fulfil his own desires over sacrificing for his country. "I understand that having a guard with you at all times impinges on your freedom, but as long as you're under my protection, you *will* walk with one."

He pulled out his phone to contact the shift manager to see what had gone wrong.

Zed stood and snatched the phone. The stare down lasted for a few seconds before his brother dropped his gaze and returned the cell.

"You need to relax, Zareb. You've amped up security twenty-fold." He swung his arm. "Everywhere I turn, there's a camera. The king wasn't happy about you stopping the palace tours for those two weeks when we first returned. You know how our father likes to show off our opulence."

Zareb snorted. Doing a thorough investigation on the tourists proved impossible, so he'd shut it down only to be vetoed when peace remained.

"Little bro, we'll be fine walking around on our own grounds without being haunted by security every minute."

The speech didn't ease the churning disquiet in his gut. Nothing had happened, and it may not come from the General, but his instincts screamed that something bad was on the way. No matter what it was, he'd protect his own.

Zed shrugged and grinned. "No one's out to kill me. The one person who might've wanted to at one point is now irrevocably in love with me."

Zareb barked out a laugh that made Nour jump. "It's a good thing, too. I'd put my money on Rio to do more harm than Bagumi's enemies any day. What are you doing here?"

Zed stepped back with his hands crossed against his chest. "You wound me, Reb. I long to be in your presence always."

Nour wound his arms around Zareb's neck and squeezed. He kissed the boy's plump cheek before tickling him under his arm. Giggles filled the room.

"Mama wants to see you."

Zareb's jaw tightened to the point of cramping. A summons from Queen Zulekha, his father's first wife, tended to give him more work because his mother was likely up to one of her infamous conspiracies.

Lately, she and the king had been insistent on him marrying. The woman would, of course, belong to a family who'd make a strong ally in times of need.

His siblings weren't setting good examples for him to maintain his bachelorhood. His sisters Amira, India, and Isha had married and claimed to be happy. He hadn't received a reason to sneak-attack any of their husbands in case they weren't treating them well.

He appreciated that he could keep an eagle eye on Amira's husband, Jake, who had moved to Bagumi. He actually missed his brother-in-law, who'd swept his wife away last week for a month-long tour of Europe before going on a cruise in the Caribbean.

Now that Zed was married and had provided their mother with her first grandchild, she'd become voracious for more. Good thing the couple were obliging with Rio already pregnant with their second one. In about six months, they'd have a crying infant in the palace again.

Zed reached for Nour, who readily went to his father. "I'm just the messenger. Save your scowls for our life-giver. She said to meet her in her suite at seven."

Zareb glanced at his watch. He had an hour. "Were you ordered to bring me in, or will she allow me the dignity of arriving by myself?"

"Nour wanted to see you after visiting with her, so I told her I'd inform you about her request. We can't go with you, anyway. Tonight, I'm spending some much-needed time with Rio as soon as I get this one to bed," Zed said with a wink.

Once again, that green-eyed monster sliced into his belly. Watching Zed with his wife and child brought up longing for a woman in his life that had snuck up on him. He didn't need it. Women were not to be trusted. Lessons learned the hard way were the ones that stuck.

"Did Mama tell you why she wanted to see me?"

Zed snorted. "And give you time to prepare?"

"Not our queen."

He'd developed the love of strategizing from her. Not everyone was privy to the insight, but his mother guided his father in many of the more important operational decisions of the country. Her opinions were valued because she saw many angles to every situation, just like the most viable piece on a chess board.

If she were head of security, no one would be able to get through her barriers because they wouldn't be able to discover how. He tried to emulate her in that regard but didn't always get it right.

"Zareb, are you okay? You seem tighter strung than usual."

He shrugged. "I'm fine."

He'd deal with the restlessness plaguing him just like he did almost everything else. By himself.

CHAPTER TWO

Malika Ahvanti adjusted the traditional heavy cotton weave top the men of her people wore, which she'd taken as the uniform in her new guise. For the thousandth time, she checked the front embroidery to ensure the flow of the garment. Along with the breast binder, it was supposed to make her meagre chest look flat so no one would guess she was a woman.

Queen Zulekha tipped her head to the side. "Stop fidgeting, dear. You must appear confident in front of my son. Weakness is his enemy."

"It's hard to do when I look like my brother instead of myself. Isn't it possible to get Prince Zareb to train me in fencing as a female? I'm good. My previous coaches can vouch for me."

"Trust me, he would refuse you."

After extensive research on her potential coach, she hadn't discovered any logical reason he didn't personally train women. "But why?"

She half-expected a growl to accompany the queen's barred teeth.

"Let's just say that he's had unpleasant experiences when it comes to working with young ladies."

If the queen had wanted her to know what had happened, she would've said it straight out. The elegant woman didn't mince words.

"I don't feel comfortable lying to him." Her stomach tightened, and she swallowed down the burning acid which rose at the thought of it. Was her goal of becoming an Olympic champion worth infuriating The Lion of Bagumi with her lie? "If he finds out that I'm deceiving him—"

"As long as you act like a surly teenage boy and don't talk too much, you'll do well. You've been practising by mimicking your brother, so you should be able to sustain the behaviour for six weeks. That's when Zareb holds an international fencing competition. Once you prove your skills in the tournament, you can reveal yourself to him."

Malika held back a sigh at the ridiculous amount of time she'd have to spend adjusting her stuffed crotch, strutting to hide her hip sway, and stopping herself from crossing her legs. She struggled not to cringe at the thought of wearing the binder when her breasts became heavy and tender before her period.

It was a good thing she'd just finished and wouldn't have to deal with it for a few more weeks. Pain killers and staying in her room braless when she wasn't working out was on the agenda for those days.

The collar of her white undershirt choked her as reality hit that in a few minutes, she was going to have to make Prince Zareb believe that she was something she wasn't. She hated herself for it, and yet, she hadn't burst out of the room, leaving apologies in her wake for having wasted the queen's time.

"You'll only have to see Zareb during training. Be careful in public areas—my son has become vigilant with having eyes on every corner of this palace."

Silence filled the room as the queen considered Malika.

"Your mother would always mention how good you were in the plays you acted in during secondary school." Queen Zulekha chuckled. "She said that your father feared that you would go into it as a profession rather than something practical. This is the same thing. Only now, it's for your future in a sport you excel at."

Malika opened her mouth to protest, but then the remembered words of her late mother brought on a full body tingle. "Promise me that you'll live life to the fullest, my darling Malika. When I look down from Heaven, I want to see you accomplish your dreams. Follow your heart and do what makes you happy."

Engaging in trickery brought her no joy, but excelling at fencing did. Living with the temporary guilt to fulfil one of her mother's last requests was what she'd do.

Queen Zulekha tipped her head the slightest bit. "To be honest, you're doing him a favour. The timing of wanting to resume your training couldn't have been more ideal. You'll be a perfect distraction in both your forms."

Before Malika could ask any of the fifteen questions that would clarify those cryptic words, a knock came on the door.

"That's Zareb. You can do this. Think about the pride you'll bring to your mother's memory when you qualify to compete in the Olympics."

It was as if the queen had read her mind and heart. She took in a deep breath before slouching on the couch with her legs open.

Show time.

***

Zareb bowed to the High Queen of Bagumi.

Seated on a gold-maroon loveseat in her suite, she offered her cheek for his kiss. He obliged before stepping back to have a more detailed look at the person he'd initially taken to be a female sharing the couch with his mother.

Delicate features of high cheekbones and a narrow-bridged nose which widened gently at the nostrils, in the middle of a slim face with no hint of stubble, had deceived him. He now looked directly at the stranger who had stood and bowed. The traditional male-style smock, a close-cut fade, and the flat chest indicated that their visitor was a young man, albeit an effeminate-looking one.

"Good evening," Zareb greeted.

"Dear heart, won't you have a seat," his mother said with a wave towards an armchair closer to her than her guest.

He struggled to maintain an indiscernible expression. The use of anything but his name meant she wanted something from him that he wouldn't readily give.

"Thank you, Mama."

He chose to sit in the centre of the couch across from the duo to best observe them.

His mother turned to the young man and touched his shoulder. "This is Maliq Sule Ahvanti. Everyone calls him Sule. Meet Prince Zareb Aamori Saene, my third child. Son of the King of Bagumi and head of security here at the palace."

Zareb's ears sharpened with interest at the pride in his mother's voice.

Sule's angled dark brown eyes stayed on him. A brush of heat licked at the back of Zareb's neck, and he raised his hand to rub it as his muscles tensed.

"It's a pleasure to meet you, Your Highness."

The young man's voice held minimal huskiness as if he hadn't yet gone through puberty. Perhaps he'd overestimated the boy's age.

Instead of responding in a like manner, Zareb tipped his head.

Sule's mouth tightened into as straight a line as a person with such full lips could achieve. His gaze never wavered as Zareb studied those feminine features. The boy's insolence intrigued him. A strong individual. Most people would be fidgeting or have looked away from his concentrated perusal.

"Sule is the child of a close friend. A sister."

He yielded to his mother's control of the stare-off by allowing himself to focus on her.

"We attended the same boarding school and had maintained our friendship ever since. Do you recall Eshe's visits here and us to her?"

"I do," he replied, remembering how happy she'd been with her friend. "You two giggled and gossiped the whole time you were together."

To his horror, his mother's eyes watered. She plucked a tissue from the box on the coffee table and dabbed the tears away before they could slide too far down her cheeks. "She was a wonderful woman."

His mother's grief when she'd heard of her friend's death had placed a pall of sorrow over the palace. Zawadi, Amira, their half-brother Zik, and his stepmother had escorted her to the funeral. The crushing empathy Zareb had felt at his mother's anguish had made it impossible for him to travel with the delegation.

He clawed fingers into a fist to keep from rubbing his chest at the lingering hurt on behalf of his mother's loss.

The grim smile she shared with Sule emphasized her heartbreak. "Four months gone, and I miss her terribly."

Sule's smooth throat bobbed with his hard swallow as his eyes glistened before he bowed his head. "She spoke highly and often of you, Your Majesty."

The heft of mourning lifted when the queen cleared her throat before clapping her hands once.

"My sweet son, my guest would like to be trained in fencing. It would give me great pleasure if you were to guide him as his personal coach."

Now she was spreading it on a little too thick. Rather than deny his mother's request outright, which would turn into a battle of wills, he decided to influence the young man to change his mind. "How old are you?"

His narrow, slumped shoulders straightened. "Eighteen."

Zareb scoffed. "What happened to your voice? You sound like a girl."

He lamented his comment at his mother's chastising gasp. She'd taught him to be dignified. It didn't do to insult her deceased friend's son.

Sule's nostrils flared for a brief moment.

"It hasn't changed yet. I've been tested, and there isn't anything medically wrong with me. I'm producing male hormones, just not enough to have me develop at the rate of my mates." He shrugged. "My father told me that his voice didn't deepen—" he touched his cheek, "—or his facial hair grow until he was a few months past eighteen. I resemble my father in many ways. This is one of them."

For the boy's sake, Zareb hoped the pre-pubescent face would harden. Unless he knew how to fight, he'd doubtlessly been teased without mercy at school for his slight frame and effeminate looks. Facial hair and broadened jaw muscles would go a long way to distinguish him as a male.

Rather than apologise for his rudeness, Zareb went on with his line of questioning. "How long have you studied fencing?"

"Four years."

"Fencing isn't a popular sport in Africa. Where did you train?"

Sule maintained eye contact. "I attended a boarding school in Spain for my education. My establishment had a club, and I joined. I topped in the competitions I participated in. When my mother became ill a year before my graduation, I returned home to be with her."

The queen patted the boy's knee.

This wasn't the time for more sentiment. "Did you finish secondary school?"

"I completed it in Loras."

"Have you started university?" Zareb asked.

Sule's gaze went to his mother for a flash before returning to him. "I don't know if I want to at this point."

Interesting manner of answering what should've been a yes or no question. After his earlier rudeness, Zareb couldn't call the young man out on whatever he was hiding. It didn't matter what secrets Sule kept— he doubted he'd be good enough to be coached directly by him to competitive stages. No matter how close the young man was to the queen, few possessed that level of skill in the sport. If the teenager wanted to join the Bagumi Fencing Team, then his other coaches could handle him; he'd wash his hands.

"Why should I train you?"

Sule shrugged as if he could care less one way or the other. A characteristic that Zareb could do without.

"I've placed in two international competitions. My last coach had high hopes of me going to the Olympics before I discontinued my training."

One of his toughest competitors throughout his career had been from Spain. "When was this?"

"A little over ten months ago."

He wouldn't have to worry about his mother's wrath when he declined to coach Sule. The request was ridiculous. "The next Olympics is two years away. You would expect me to train you within this time after you've taken all of those months off? Do you think I'm some kind of sorcerer?"

The twitch of Sule's eye proved the only indication of annoyance as his voice came out smooth and controlled.

"Knowing how much I loved and missed the sport, at my mother's request, my father built me a small training facility." He clasped then unclasped his hands, resting them on his knees. "As you may or may not know, Loras is a beautiful coastal territory, and we get many foreigners visiting. I never lacked a sparring partner. This allowed me to maintain my skills."

"Why not go back to Madrid to train with the coach that thinks you have such great potential?"

The queen glared at Zareb. "Watch your tone, young man. This isn't an interrogation. Sule is my guest. Accord him some respect."

At twenty-eight, he should be able to stand up to his mother. Maybe he'd develop the skill when he turned fifty.

"I apologise if I offended you," he grit out. Keeping the peace with his mother was worth relinquishing that small bit of his pride.

Sule dipped his chin. "It's all right. I trained in Barcelona, not Madrid. I don't want to venture too far away from my home again. If I work with you here in Bagumi, I can easily return to visit my family, or they can come here. My father feels better knowing that I'm accessible. And besides …" His cheeks rose in a smile, revealing bright, straight teeth which made him appear even more feminine. "You're an Olympic individual bronze medallist in épée, which happens to be the style I prefer."

Zareb's brow lifted a fraction, but he remained quiet. Appeasing his curiosity over why Sule had chosen épée over foil or sabre wouldn't help get rid of the young man any faster.

Sule's voice was filled with awe as he continued. "You're the first African to ever earn the distinction of winning an Olympic medal in fencing at the Olympics. I aim to be the second. It would be an honour to be coached by you."

Zareb's chest puffed out, but the boy's flattery wouldn't get him into his gym.

His mother held up a hand. "Before you make a decision, will you please do this old woman a favour and spin with him?"

"I believe you mean spar," he corrected.

His mother's light giggle had him blinking to ensure the source.

"It was on the tip of my tongue. Now that it's settled, Sule, go to your room and get your gear. My son will take you to the gym and put you through your paces. I'm sure you'll impress him with your skills. If you can take his ego down a notch or two by scoring, I would be grateful."

Once again, the master strategist had won this battle, but he wouldn't allow her to defeat him. He'd end up sending this young pup back to Loras, where he belonged.

Zareb shot off a text message. "One of my guards will escort you to the gym."

"Thank you." Sule stood and bowed before leaving the room.

He was about to go, too, when his mother held up a hand to stop him.

She got to her feet and approached to sit at his side. "I made a vow to Sule's mother before she died that I would do whatever I could to help her family. I won't let good talent go to waste, not when you can groom it."

"I can't make any promises just because you did."

"I know, Zareb. I'm just asking you to give Sule a chance. After all the gloating that Eshe has done about Sule's talents over the years, I believe we might have another Olympic champion in our midst."

The enthusiasm with which his mother spoke lit a spark of excitement. Could Sule be the one he'd been looking to mentor? He wouldn't hold his breath. It took a whole lot more than a mother's pride in their child's ability and accomplishment to make it into the Olympics. Sacrifice, discipline, dedication, strength, and a genuine love for performing and living the sport.

"If I find him lacking, I won't train him."

"I'm sure you'll be surprised at the talent you discover."

Zareb got to his feet, ready to leave.

"Darling?"

One side of his nose flared before he turned to give her his attention. "Yes, Mama?"

A sweet smile graced her face. "Do your best to not be difficult to Sule."

He held in a grunt at her request, knowing how it would go down.

CHAPTER THREE

Malika had held onto her temper with all the restraint her athletic five-foot-six frame could muster. Zareb had turned out to be an arrogant, insolent, stubborn man. How unlike the sweet, quiet boy she'd met when she'd been seven and him ten. The memory of him helping her to her feet and dusting off her knobby knees when she'd tripped in her attempt to keep up with the older boys had been embedded.

She winced as she tightened the specialized plastic chest protector with more force than necessary. The equipment had been designed to flatten her chest like a man's while providing her with both comfort, agility, and protection.

For the hundredth time, she questioned if the guilt-inducing ruse of posing as a teenage boy was necessary. Or even safe. Queen Zulekha thought so. But then again, the woman was also under the far-fetched impression that Malika would wed her youngest son one day. The queen had brought up the time her seven-year-old self had announced that she wanted to marry Zareb when they grew up.

It brought back the memories of when Malika had returned home during her mother's illness. There had been several occasions when she'd mentioned conversations with the queen. The two women had concluded that it would be great to merge their families through marriage. She'd grinned at the nostalgia in her mother's voice but had seen it as just a fancy on their part.

It wasn't until the queen brought up the potential of her getting to know Zareb on a more personal level as they'd discussed 'Operation Sule' that she'd realized the older women had been serious.

Her lips vibrated at the force of the air she blew out. That was never going to happen, especially after meeting the prince as an adult. He was much too cold to be a good husband to her. Her list of qualities included caring, affection, and most of all, respect in communication.

To his credit, he'd listened, even if she could see the doubt in his eyes. He was no fool. She'd been shocked that he hadn't seen right through her male costume to the woman beneath. But then again, people had often confused her and her younger brother Maliq when they'd been teenagers, so maybe her playing a young man wasn't as far-fetched as she'd thought.

She knew for a fact that she wouldn't be falling into any kind of long-term relationship with Prince Zareb that didn't involve a sword. Going off into fling territory didn't sound so bad, though. The man knew how to wear his confidence to the point of making her knees weak. Considering that she was sitting down when it had happened, he exuded some potent sex appeal.

She'd always been a glutton for a tall man who possessed the stunning gorgeousness of a muscular warrior statue. When he'd walked into the queen's apartment, her mouth had gone dry at the combination of sharp cheekbones, full firm lips, and piercing brown eyes. Adding in that thick head of gorgeous locs had snatched the breath right out of her.

She could handle ogling him, but getting involved was out of the question.

The singular goal of training under a coach who could get her to the Olympics without moving far from her family sat firmly in her grasp. She hadn't lied to him about her objective, although there'd been a major deviation when it came to the timeframe of her past. She'd initiated her training while in boarding school in Barcelona. Her skills had earned her a full scholarship to The University of Notre Dame in the United States, where she'd won her way through competitions on the path to the Olympics.

A month after graduation, her mother had been diagnosed with an aggressive form of ovarian cancer. She'd dropped everything and gone back home, losing her spot with the coach when she hadn't returned after six months. She'd chosen her priority. Being at her mother's side when she'd most needed her had been the best choice. The only one.

Would the distress of her heart being crushed at the loss of her mother ever go away? She blinked back the burn from her eyes. This wasn't the time. She had a hard-headed man to impress.

His misogynistic philosophy of not training women was unacceptable. The queen had motivated her to return to fencing and to do so with Zareb as her coach. She'd decided to prove that women were just as good as men in the sport. He had no right to abstain from working with women. The glitch being that she wouldn't be able to reveal it until later.

The niggling thought that he had a valid reason for his decision pulsed.

The feminist in her shut down the rational thought. It didn't make it right to exclude a whole gender from his training regime.

Dressed in white high-tech fencing regalia from neck to feet, Malika felt much more comfortable than she had sitting in the queen's large, ornate living room in her costume of trousers and a thick black and white, flaring traditional smock over a white T-shirt.

Thank goodness the prince hadn't been in the same locker room with her. She would've had to come up with an excuse for why she'd changed in the shower stall.

She smoothed a hand over the hair she'd had cut a few millimetres shy of looking shaved on the sides and back. The top left slightly longer.

The loss of hair had been a welcome change. She'd always preferred it short. As she'd grown older, she'd worn it longer to fit in with her friends and make her boyfriends happy. At twenty-five, she was once again free to display it as short as she wanted. It didn't make up for how wretched she felt about being a liar, but at least, it wasn't all bad.

She adjusted the cup in her pants which created the slight bulge that gave credence to her persona. How could men stand having something so uncomfortable between their legs?

She smirked as the silly thought eased a bit of her anxiety.

But procrastinating wouldn't get her a coach. Taking in a deep inhale to boost her courage, she picked up her mask and gloves from the bench. Collecting her épée with her free hand, she kissed the sword for good luck as she'd done in the past before competitions.

I don't have to beat him. Just exhibit my potential to be a champion.

Ensuring that her stride lacked any sway, she left the locker room to face down The Lion of Bagumi.

***

As Zareb warmed up, the training space buzzed. The busybodies were focused on him and who he'd be fencing with rather than on their own practice.

He didn't blame them for their interest. As a spectacular fighter, he impressed even himself when he watched the videos of his matches. With the combination of height, speed, and the ability to foresee his opponent's moves, he'd been unstoppable. Then he'd injured his hamstring during a practice session. Rather than let it heal for the proper amount of time, he'd competed in a match that he'd been scheduled for.

His concept of invincibility had worsened the injury. Three months of healing had passed when his father had had a severe heart attack. On the edge of death, the king had made him swear to protect the family at all cost. Without hesitation, he'd agreed.

Since he couldn't do both with the passion that he applied to what he dedicated himself to, he'd given up any further dreams of attaining the gold in the next Olympic games. The pain and regret of losing what he loved loomed like a shadow in his heart. It perpetually reminded him that he'd never know how great he could've been.

And now, he was on the search for someone to train as a way of vicariously regaining his own personal glory. He had strong doubts that Sule would lead him down that path. How had he let his mother stronghold him into fighting this small boy? No matter. He'd wipe the floor with him and send him packing.

Out came his current source of annoyance from the locker room.

"Are you familiar with wireless fencing?" he asked when Sule had reached him.

A muscle twitched in the young man's jaw, but his calm tone belied his apparent irritation. "I am. It's the technology we used at my training facility. We can see if my gear is compatible with your equipment."

Impressed, he nodded, narrowing his eyes into a stern glower. "Good. We're going to use it to do the scoring."

His attempt at intimidating his opponent seemed to fail when Sule didn't look away.

"After all," he continued. "We want this to be fair. Completely objective and impartial."

Sule's minuscule head bow seemed more of a taunt than a sign of acknowledgement. "Of course, Your Highness. Is it okay if I take a moment to warm up?"

"Go ahead." He wouldn't want the boy to use it as an excuse when he trounced him.

Zareb had arranged for one of the coaches to referee and another to monitor the scoring. After being programmed into the computer, the system would register when the opponent's uniform was hit, garnering a point. One of his coaches connected Sule's blade to the equipment and found it successful at capturing a touch.

From the opposite end of the strip, Zareb observed the young man preparing for the match with active stretches and various practice techniques. Although the adept movements demonstrated Sule's familiarity with the sport, it didn't mean he could fence well.

Mask on and épée in hand, the boy stepped forward until he reached the en garde line.

Zareb followed suit. They each raised their sword in salute, slid their masks on, and got into position, ready to fight.

Although he didn't consider this a real match, his muscles flexed with the anticipation of competing. As they waited for the referee to start the bout, he strategized how he'd quickly get the points so he could shut down the nonsense idea of this young man training under his private tutelage.

Zareb assessed Sule's stance and found no fault in it. The épée was steady in his hand.

When the referee told them to begin, Zareb advanced. Sule retreated with two quick steps, keeping the distance between them. Then just as soon as Sule stopped his movement, he transitioned into the aggressor and advanced with the same two steps he'd shuffled backwards with. He added another before lunging in an attempt to strike Zareb in the thigh.

If he hadn't been quick in blocking with his épée as he shuffled out of the way, Sule would've scored a point.

Notable, but probably just luck.

When Zareb had first been introduced to fencing in junior high school, he'd attempted all three styles. Although he excelled at foil and sabre, he enjoyed épée most. He found a thrill in defending his whole body from head to toe from getting struck by an opponent's blade.

Being a larger man than Sule, he had the advantage of distance which he now utilized to drive the boy back before landing a strike on his shoulder. The scoring machine beeped, indicating a solid hit. The crowd clapped.

Returning to the en garde line, he took notice of the motionless spectators. The show would be over soon, and he'd be able to tell his mother that Sule didn't have what it took to work with him. He'd be sure to offer him a chance to train in his facility.

Zareb once again took the offensive, this time going in for the kill. The boy stepped forward, shortening the distance between them, blocking Zareb's strike. Sule exploded into a lunge and struck Zareb's rib. The loud shrill noise went off.

He'd been scored. A clean, swift, honest point that it took far too long for him to mentally register.

Not a sound could be heard in the building. Perhaps because his ears had filled with the blood rushing to his head. Or the crowd was just as shocked as him by his opponent's victorious strike. The stunning moment over, they let out a wild roar of applause.

Sule had utilized the tactic of infighting. An excellent way for a shorter individual to score, although it increased his chances of being hit.

Back to each of their respective start lines, they faced off again. Perhaps it was cockiness that made Sule advance first this time. Zareb easily took himself out of the boy's striking range. He'd only needed to learn that lesson once. Careful not to underestimate him again, he shifted forward. Sule retreated with a speed that could only come from both skill and excessive practice.

Zareb attacked Sule's abdomen. The young man parried, depriving him of a point. Advancing again, this time, he lunged before his opponent could step back, striking him in the arm. The buzzer sounded.

Fast and light-footed, Sule came close to scoring once more as they sparred. The underestimation of the boy's talent was what had won the one strike that had gotten past Zareb. Elevating his game to competition level for the rest of the three-minute round, he made quick work of gaining the winning points.

Victory was his. But he couldn't overlook how good Sule was. To score against an Olympic medallist was no small feat. Yet, it had been accomplished on this day by a yet-to-fully mature young man.

CHAPTER FOUR

Malika wrestled with her energetic spirit to keep from running around the locker room, leaping on and over benches. She didn't have the time, so she appeased the celebration of her scoring against the great Zareb Saene with a short dance in the empty space before jogging to the stall, peeling out of her sweaty fencing uniform and taking a quick shower.

The nastiness of sitting in Zareb's office funky and uncomfortable outweighed the risk of being discovered as a woman. After towelling dry, she bound her breasts by wiggling into the black vest-style binder, which gave her a flat-chested look while allowing her flexibility of movement. It helped that she just filled a size A cup.

She shoved the T-shirt and smock over her head and rushed out to verify the news that he'd accepted her as his student. He couldn't say no after her aggressive score. So, what if he'd trounced her for the rest of the match?

The moment he'd found her to be an actual threat, lightning couldn't have struck faster, as unexpectedly, or with more force than Zareb during the rest of their duel. The beatdown had been the best experience of her fencing career.

She'd gain so much from him. She couldn't wait to be on the giving end of some of the moves he'd whipped her with. For such a large man, he had the speed and agility of someone her size. This shouldn't have been a surprise after how often she'd watched videos of him fencing. Experiencing it first-hand had been the most extraordinary experience of her life.

Was she getting ahead of herself by presuming Zareb would train her? How could he not? She wasn't as good as him yet. But under his guidance, she could bring more prestige to Africa in the name of fencing.

All she had to do was work her behind off and keep the aspect of being a female hidden. She packed her gear in the gym bag, making sure to place the chest protector at the bottom. Tempted to let the jock strap hang outside of the bag, she laughed as she stuffed it in.

Now that she was embroiled in the deception, she had no choice but to keep up the masculine façade. The guilt was ever-present, but everything would work out. Attaining her dreams relied heavily on her acting skills. Six weeks would pass by in a blink. Behaving like a teenage boy had to be easier than being a twenty-five-year-old woman.

***

Zareb stiffened at the knock on his office door.

"Come in," he barked.

Expecting the young man to strut into the room, he was surprised that Sule maintained the same stride he'd had when entering the gym. No arrogance touched him.

The flick of his hand indicated that Sule should sit. The younger man dropped into a chair and slid down with his legs spread as if he were in his living room.

Sule's face was familiar. Perhaps it came from the fact that he'd played with the boy's older siblings when he'd been younger.

"Sit up straight."

Insolence flashed in the boy's eyes before he took his time to raise his body.

Zareb attempted to infuse some intimidation into the conversation by glowering. "How did you find the session?"

"It was cool. Getting to spar with you was a privilege. Thank you for the audition."

No mention of his scored point. "What's one thing you learned?"

Sule leaned forward. "It's not something new, but because I'm on the shorter side, if I'm to be a champion, I have to be able to do more infighting, which would help even if my opponent is my own height."

The slight hair growth on Zareb's cheeks released a rasping sound as he rubbed it. "Getting inside your competitor's guard would be the best way for you to earn points. You'd have to increase your speed, defence and add more agility. Your endurance declined after the first minute. It must be rectified."

He searched the young man for a reaction. Other than the look of boredom, which he'd found to be a natural occurrence in the teenagers he'd encountered, he detected nothing.

Now came the part that should elicit a response.

"You have a great deal of potential, but you've got a long way to go in order to consider yourself an Olympic hopeful." He picked up a pen and pointed it at the still emotionless Sule. "You'll train six days a week. A *minimum* of four hours in the early morning and four in the afternoon. Your day off will be Sunday. I'll set a schedule, but I won't be with you every minute. To survive this program, you must exhibit discipline, physical and mental strength, and determination."

He glared at Sule, who maintained eye contact. No smile at the prospect of training under him to fulfil his dreams or groan of frustration about the work involved. The boy was like him in more than his skill and aptitude for greatness as a fencer. He might be the protégé he'd been waiting so long for.

"Do you agree with what I've just explained is expected of you?"

"Yes." Sule paused and added, almost begrudgingly, "Your Highness. I'm ready to do anything to become a champion."

Only time would tell how much Sule would be willing to sacrifice once training began.

"For the first two weeks, I'll be your main coach in the early mornings. You'll be under the care of Coach Olu and Coach Dorna for the afternoon sessions. If you miss one, I'll kick you out." He levelled a stern, narrow-eyed gaze. "Am I making myself clear?"

"Perfectly, Your Highness. Thank you for the opportunity to work with you and your team. I know I'll learn a lot and go far. I won't disappoint you."

"Good. Meet me here at four in the morning. Wear running shoes because we'll go for at least a five-mile jog to help increase your endurance. Make sure to bring your fencing gear, too."

Zareb almost allowed himself to smile when Sule's eyes widened. Not sure if it was the prospect of having to be up at four or the jog that caused the look of surprise to slip from his controlled demeanour. He'd find out tomorrow.

"And another thing. You'll fill the time between sessions by continuing your education. Find an online course at one of the universities in Bagumi and report back to me so we can get you registered."

Zareb rubbed his nose to hide the unsolicited grin at Sule's dropped jaw. There was no idling at the palace. When the young man wasn't fencing or learning about it, he'd elevate his educational status.

"I'll see you tomorrow. Don't be late," he snapped before picking up his tablet and returning to work.

CHAPTER FIVE

The struggle to catch enough oxygen into her lungs to survive had been a supreme hardship as the sadist set a gruelling pace. Malika would rather have a foot severed than admit that their morning run would be the death of her. She'd stayed by Zareb's side, although it didn't take being a genius to realize that he'd slowed his pace for her.

Not that she wouldn't mind falling back to scrutinize his tight behind and thick shredded legs emphasized by shorts that stopped mid-thigh. His black tank top showing off defined muscles under enticing chocolate-brown skin had her taking an extra drink of water at their four a.m. meet up.

She'd shaken off the need to ogle. Her mission took precedence over being tempted by a tall, fit, and unbelievably handsome man. Even his slightly off-centred nose appealed. She'd forced her determined hands to abstain from reaching out to touch his perfection every time she saw him. Nothing she could do about the belly flips, though.

She may not be a male, but she was supposed to be acting like one. Groping the prince wouldn't be tolerated. The man brooked no nonsense. Malika doubted that inappropriate staring and touching would be accepted even if he knew she was a woman.

Day Four, and she hadn't missed a single session. She'd undergone intense physical training all of her life. In her younger years, she'd taken gymnastics, ballet, and tennis. As a teenager, she'd gotten interested in football. Although she loved the sport, she didn't excel at it. It wasn't until she'd tried fencing that she'd learned how to push herself to the outer limits of what she knew she could achieve.

Due to the downpour of rain that morning, they'd run on the indoor track.

Just before the last lap, Zareb turned to her. "Sprint full out for this last round, and you'll skip running tomorrow. If you don't give it your all, you'll have an extra mile in the morning."

Challenge accepted because she really had no choice in the matter, she geared up for the sprint while waiting for him to give the signal. When he yelled, "Go!" she sped off.

She focused on pumping her arms, contracting her core, and putting one foot in front of the other with haste. Her legs stretched to the limit so that her sneakers barely touched the floor as she surged forward.

He'd joined the contest and sped past her. When she reached the finish point an eternity later, she shifted into a walk several metres after her legs had decided to reduce their speed. The binder felt as if it had tightened, and she struggled to breathe. Gulping in air, she closed her eyes and held her arms up to get rid of the cramp, making her wish she no longer had ribs. All she wanted to do was rip the binder off to ease the pressure. That would make a fine impression on her new coach.

When she opened her lids, Zareb was observing her. That glorious head of locs cocked to the side meant trouble.

She lowered her arms and looked down to see if everything was in place. A flat chest met her vision, and she sighed with relief. "Side cramp."

"Are you okay?"

Her jaw dropped, and her feet stuck to the track. Was this an act of actual caring from the apathetic prince?

"Yeah. It's getting better."

"Keep moving."

Able to inhale again without the sensation of a knife twisting in her ribs, she asked, "So, no run?"

The brisk nod set off her grin.

He did a double-take, and his gaze lingered. The stony expression relaxed the slightest bit. "It must make you happy not to have to run tomorrow. You never smile."

Her sweaty skin became even hotter at the direct concentrated attention. She hated how she liked being close enough to see the minuscule mole under his right eye. It was wrong to want to caress those sculpted muscles. To desire to be held in those powerful arms as she lost herself against his hard body.

Every once in a while, as they'd trained, she'd caught him staring at her. During those times, tingles sizzled down her spine. She'd gotten the sense that he was assessing her on a personal level rather than as a coach. Did he sense the electrical currents between them?

Of course, he didn't!

To him, she was a young man. Not only that, but ten years his junior. Even if he liked being with men, he would never go for someone as young as he thought Sule was. Technically legal, yet still a teenager.

She ripped her eyes away and set her mouth into a straight line. "It's not the reward that makes me happy, but the fact that I gave everything to that sprint, and you recognized it."

"Down to the weight room. We'll get some more muscle on you before the month is through." He tossed her a quick look over his shoulder. "If you last that long."

This prince certainly knew how to make a person feel deserving.

***

Every day for the past two weeks, Zareb had become more impressed with Sule's endurance of the exhaustive training he'd put him through. Perhaps the young man's dream was the most important thing in his life, after all. Sule had spent the time improving himself and had not only absorbed the information he was given but implemented and utilized it in the correct manner and at the right time.

Zareb had seen the raw talent when they'd first sparred, but now that it had been honed a little, he knew Sule would be as great a fencer as he'd been in his prime, if not better.

He wouldn't hold the fact that the boy was a bit effeminate against him. To his trained eye, Sule's walk would change to include more of a hip swing, especially when he was tired.

His skin had prickled on the couple of occasions he'd caught Sule fixated on him with those dark, angular eyes. Not as if amazed at a mentor, but almost as if in a state of longing. It made him query the boy's sexuality. Which would make sense considering what he'd observed of the young man's features and occasional mannerisms. Not that it was any of his business as long as the youngster maintained his respectful nature.

A chill drove down his spine, causing a full-body shiver as he recalled the unexpected dip in his stomach when he'd caught one of Sule's rare smiles. Full lips had raised, revealing glimmering white teeth. The expression had called to him to respond in kind, which he'd resisted. For a disturbing moment, he'd wanted to reach out to stroke the smooth skin and features that made him look more like a female than a male.

Zareb shook his head so hard that his bound locs smacked his cheek. He couldn't be attracted to the boy who reminded him more of a girl than his own sister at that age.

No! Attraction wasn't the issue here. The one thing he'd mastered in this world was knowing and being himself.

He'd been attracted to women all of his life. The thought of being with a man hadn't crossed his mind, not even on the occasions when guys had tried to come on to him. He hadn't been inclined to accept what they'd been offering. World-travelled and educated about varying sexualities, he'd rebuffed them gently but with a stern honesty that had left them understanding where he stood on the matter.

He accepted people for who they were, but without a doubt, he recognized himself as heterosexual.

Then what was happening with Sule? Could he be attracted to someone of the same sex after all these years? His gut quivered as he struggled with the newfound thought. How could that be? Was he bisexual? Gay? Sexually fluid or whatever term was floating around these days? What the hell was going on with him?

He ran a calloused palm over his face as confusion and uncertainty like he'd never felt before wracked his brain. Fear held its place, too. He hadn't been with a woman in months. Perhaps he'd forgotten what true attraction was, and this was just …

Something that had occurred as a fleeting reaction because he was proud of his new student for working so hard. For being like him. Someone to groom into winning the gold medal like he hadn't been able to.

Not only was Sule a fellow male, but he was ten years his junior. Ten years!

At the age of eighteen, he'd still been a child. Others in his culture might disagree. For him, such a large age gap at his tender age was unacceptable, even if Sule had been a young lady.

He hung his head.

And yet, he'd reacted to Sule in a way that proved disturbing. He rested his head on his chair as his thoughts looped back around to why. It had to be the fact that he appreciated Sule possessing the kind of drive and potential to bring further eminence to not just their continent but to him.

The boy reminded him of himself, and appreciated no one's company more than he did his own. It must've translated onto Sule.

That had to be it. It was the only explanation he'd accept, so he ended the contemplation.

CHAPTER SIX

"Thanks, everyone. Great meeting," Malika said to the faces on her laptop. "See you same time next week. In the meantime, keep me updated on your progress."

Four computer programmers of her IT consultancy group said their goodbyes before logging off. Her business partner, Shoshana Anderson, stayed on the line. They'd set up their IT consultancy three years ago and were now reaping the benefits with an increased client base and employee list. It felt good to see the huge loan they'd taken out decreasing with each monthly payment. It wouldn't be long before every cent of their profits went into their pockets.

She'd forever be grateful to her mother for more than her generous love. The business-savvy woman had made the suggestion of Malika starting her own company when she'd had difficulty finding an appropriate job after graduating from university. With no sponsor to pay for her fencing training, she'd needed a way to accomplish her goal. Equipment and quality coaching were expensive, and she couldn't rely on her parents to support her forever. For once, she'd listened to her mother. The venture had threatened to plummet into nothingness during the initial stages. Still, with her best friend from college shoring them up with both her IT and management expertise, things had gotten better.

And now, she sat in Bagumi training under a world-renowned fencing champion while still being able to handle her company. Life was good.

"How's the preparation for your parents' anniversary dinner coming?" Malika asked.

Shoshana's mass of curly hair shook, framing her deep golden-brown skin. "Don't even ask. My mother is on my back about it. It turns out that thirty years of being married to the same man without suffocating him in his sleep is a big damn deal."

Malika laughed. "I'd say it is. Why don't you hire a party planner?"

"I like hanging out with my mother these days. It's as if I've finally woken up to how great she—" Shoshana's onyx eyes rounded. "Oh, Malika. I'm so sorry."

In an attempt to downplay the depth that the loss of her mother had dug into her, she waved down a hand. "It's okay to appreciate your mom. She's an amazing woman. Tell her I said hello, and I miss her."

Shoshana looked away from the screen for a moment before pasting on a smile. "Um, I will. Tell me what's going on with you."

"Not much. Still training."

"With a gorgeous fencer who happens to be a prince." She fanned her face. "How do you stand it?"

Malika raised a brow. "Have you forgotten that he thinks I'm a dude?"

Shoshana chuckled. "I kinda did. How's that going?"

"He hasn't kicked me out of the program yet, so I must be doing something right."

Her friend clicked her teeth. "I can't believe that he can get away with not training women."

It didn't sit right to have other people question Zareb's Neanderthal ways. Just because she wasn't privy to why he'd made his decision didn't mean there wasn't a good reason behind it.

"It's like Quest Technologies accepting the clients we work with. We choose based on what we can offer. Maybe he does the same."

"Huh. Still sounds wrong."

Malika didn't disagree. "How are things with Jonathan? Will I be having to fly out for a wedding sometime soon?"

"Ha. That man is as far from proposing as I am to eating ice cream without blowing up the place."

Malika burst out laughing, glad that she could be herself with an old friend. "Why don't you take the leap and ask him?"

"No way! It's a risk I'm not ready to take. What if he said no? You know I don't do well with rejection." She sighed. "I've been dropping some not subtle hints, so he knows that I'm ready to take the plunge. He's a smart man. He'll come around."

"I hope so. You deserve to be happy."

Shoshana smiled. "I already am."

"Awww."

Malika's heart sighed, wanting what her friend had. She wouldn't mention it to Shoshana until after the event, but she'd soon get the chance to meet Zareb as her true feminine self. The queen had insisted that she attend the celebration of the anniversary of the king's enthronement tonight. Her appearance as Sule would be short-lived, but then, Malika would stay for the duration of the ball.

What a difference working with him had made in getting to see a deeper level. Although he was nobody's teddy bear, she'd discovered that he wasn't as hard as he presented himself. He'd always been respectful to Sule, if not brisk. She'd witnessed him speaking to a couple of his gym members during her afternoon sessions, and he'd been personable. Despite the intensity of the workouts, there hadn't been a session that she'd wanted to end because it meant leaving him. There was also the way her heart banged in her chest every time they got together. That had to be some kind of a sign.

It was time to find out if she and Zareb were as suited as the queen insisted.

Who was she kidding? Thoughts about being with him in her true form intruded into her mind when she should be focused on creating codes for her clients or engaging in conversations at the dinner table.

Would he be interested in Malika the way she was him? If he was, would she be willing to forget her dreams of fencing greatness by telling him the truth so that they could be together with no lies between them? Only time would tell.

***

With the party a few feet away, Zareb wished he could head in the opposite direction to avoid the mass of people. Tonight, as they did every year, they would raise a toast to the king and let him know how beloved he truly was.

He reached the security detail performing a second check of identification and invitations at the massive carved Bubinga wood doors. Most of his crew were on duty this evening. Like him, as always, they were armed and ready for any eventuality. The guest list of names the two queens had given him had been thoroughly vetted, so things should run smoothly.

No use asking if there had been any issues—he'd have already heard about it in his earpiece. With a sigh of resignation, he stepped into the crystalline paradise the queens had created. He'd make his presence known for an hour, no longer, before leaving to keep an eye on the festivities at a non-engaging yet close distance.

The plucked notes of guitars, blending with the cool melody of a keyboard and the rhythmic beats of a traditional skin drum, met him as he entered. Striding through the room in search of his mother, he kept his attention on the visitors as he ignored the stares from some of the more curious. He preferred to keep to the background, so it was rare for people to encounter him.

The area could seat two hundred at dinner tables, but his mother had opted for a standing room gathering with a few seats along the periphery. Something different for her. Perhaps it was so she could pack more people into the space. A rough guess would place the head count at close to four hundred versus the five hundred that had been invited.

Zawadi came into view. His oldest brother touched the tips of his finger to his palm in a silent call. When Zareb reached the crown prince, Zawadi flicked his wrist in a dismissal of his security detail.

The man glanced at Zareb. When he nodded, the guard backed away.

Zawadi's dark eyes blazed. "No more."

"It's necessary. I have this sense of apprehension, and it's not clear why."

"A bodyguard around the clock is not required."

Zareb clenched his jaw. The discussion had been ongoing. He knew his overprotectiveness wasn't the best, but he needed his family safe until he figured out why his instincts had been firing. He hadn't been able to discover anything.

Zawadi laid a hand on his shoulder and squeezed. "I know you've got everything covered. You always have. My brother, I'm not asking for much. Just my freedom back. You know I can take care of myself."

Zawadi was right. They'd both trained to be officers at the Royal Military Academy, Sandhurst. His time at the institution had been spent living in the shadow his big brother's perfection had cast.

Zareb considered Zawadi. He needed to let go of his own insecurities and let his family live. Whatever his gut was trying to tell him would materialize. Hopefully, he'd be able to prevent anything horrible from happening, but he was making everyone miserable with his mother-hen protection. Their happiness was the most important thing.

"I'll ease up."

Zawadi let his arm drop to his side. "Not just for me, but everyone."

"Fine. But when you leave the palace walls, security will be tight."

"Agreed."

Zareb would get the last win. "Starting tomorrow."

This got a chuckle from his stoic brother. "Stop by my place next week, and we'll hang out. It's been a while."

The simple invitation from a man he respected pleased him. "I'd like that."

Zareb signalled to the guard to return.

"Try to enjoy the party," Zawadi said with a mischievous glimmer in his eyes.

"I see that you're sense of humour is intact."

His brother left, laughing.

Zareb zoned in on the most elegant woman in the room. She was in her element, surrounded by her admirers. His sisters had been disappointed to give their regrets at not being able to attend. Otherwise, his mother's grace, regality, and beauty would have had true competition. He found the idea of her organizing the party on a date that his sisters wouldn't be able to steal attention from her intriguing. Not even she was that manipulative.

Or was she?

He waited on the outside of the crowd until his mother noticed his arrival and nodded.

When the people saw who she'd given her attention to, they divided, allowing him to pass through. He bent to place a kiss on her proffered cheek. The solid man of a guard he'd assigned to her shifted to relieve the uneasiness of not having a wall to his back.

His mother beamed. "You made it."

"Did you think I wouldn't?" Or had a choice?

She reached for his hand and led him forward. "Between you and Isha, I'm not sure which is more stubborn. I can never tell what either of you is going to do at any given moment."

He and his eldest half-sister had definitive ways of seeing the world and acted accordingly. They didn't always agree. It was oftentimes the peacemaker of the family, India, who had the courage and charm to separate them during their more heated arguments. If Isha didn't come home soon, he'd have to visit her.

The large gathering was already starting to get to him. "I won't be able to stay long."

"I figured as much. I'd like you to meet someone." She craned her Bagumi-gold, diamond, and ruby-jewelled neck as she searched the area. "Now, where is she?"

His mother was once again on a mission to set him up. He wouldn't fall for it. "Out of all these people, you want me to meet one?"

Her laughter came out as a contagious tinkle, and the corner of his lips tipped upward.

"She'll be more than enough."

He continued to scan the room for anything out of the ordinary. Anyone who appeared inebriated would be escorted out before they had the chance to make trouble.

"Where's Baba?"

"If you hadn't been tardy, you would've witnessed him having a wonderful time. He left a short while before you entered to make a wardrobe change." She tilted her head to look up at him. "Your drama-king of a father wanted to change into four outfits this evening. I talked him down to two; otherwise, he would've spent the whole night dressing rather than enjoying this spectacular party Sapphire, and I organized."

He glanced around to find his stepmother. The queen caught his eye and smiled. He returned the gesture, making a mental note to speak with her before disappearing.

"Your father will be back soon, so don't leave until then."

He looked at his mother. "We spoke in his quarters this morning."

He liked the changes that had overcome his father since his heart attack a couple of years ago. In his eyes, he'd become a nicer man. A transformation had come over Zareb, too. For the first time, he'd realized that his father wouldn't always be with him.

They hadn't gotten along for the majority of his life. Two headstrong men in the same household was never a good combination. Where his brothers had been born with the gift of tact or charm, the traits had skipped him. The verbal and behavioural filters had come later in life. Almost too late to have appreciated the man he'd butted heads with more than he should've.

Time and experience had taught Zareb to be more tolerant of others and yielding to the power they held in their own right. The threat of losing the man who had taught him that important lesson through example had made him appreciative of the king. No matter how strained their relationship may have been in the past, he wanted to know his father better while he could.

He'd given up his goal of returning to the Olympics when his father had asked him to take care of his family. As heavy as it made his heart feel at times, he'd never regret the decision.

His mother's warm hand rested against his forearm. "Always the dutiful son."

"He deserves nothing less."

"This is true, my cocoa pod sweetness." Once again, her gaze swept the room. "Where could she be?"

In the middle of hoping that the mystery guest would remain lost, his attention caught on Sule's face between the branches of a potted palm. He shivered at the unguarded initial impulse to go to the young man. Venomous spiders scurrying along his skin couldn't have made him any more uncomfortable at the realization.

He had a lot to sort out.

CHAPTER SEVEN

Malika rested a hand against her roiling stomach as terror threatened to have her drop and curl up on the floor of the alcove she cowered in.

Zareb's presence in the crowded room had eradicated any illusion that she could go through with meeting him as her female self. Despite her having to lie to him because of his sexist philosophy, she liked him as a person, and this scared the confidence right out of her. And to be fair, she'd only seen him be respectful to the women he'd encountered while in her presence. She could've been knocked over with her own sword when she'd learned that he didn't directly train women, but he allowed them to use his gym and be coached by other members of his team.

His lean, muscular build and stunning handsomeness, that she had to force her gaze away from when they trained, added to the getting-longer-list of things she appreciated about him.

She chewed on the inside of her cheek. He thought she was a guy. Things wouldn't turn out well when he discovered the truth, especially after meeting her as Malika. She wasn't trying to play him for a fool, only get the chance to become the best in fencing. Getting to know him on a personal level would convey otherwise.

Yet, the queen insisted that she meet him tonight as the vagina-toting Malika. Whatever Queen Zulekha requested, she got. So here she was, trying to figure out a way out of the situation without infuriating Her Majesty.

The distance to any of the exits combined with her screaming muscles held her in place. For the past few days, she'd been coached by Zareb's assistants. Today, he'd decided to cram ten hours of training into a four-hour morning workout.

She considered herself lucky that the prince rarely showed up in the evenings. The multitudes of pushups, squats and weight repetitions had left her arms and legs feeling limp and lifeless after an exhaustive run on the palace grounds. The great part was that it had taken less effort to keep up with him compared to their first day of training.

Slinking deeper behind the plant into the nook as she noticed not only the queen but Zareb scanning the room, she came to the conclusion that she couldn't go through with it.

Why had she listened to the queen?

Because you want a chance to get to know Zareb outside the fencing world.

As a woman.

If she couldn't be honest with him, she could at least be so with herself.

A couple strolled past. The suspicious staring had her standing straight and touching the plant as if assessing what kind of species it was. She either had to garner the courage to talk to the prince as Malika or—

Well, there was no other option.

She smoothed the full-length skirt of her hunter-green and silver off-the-shoulder silk dress. With a nod to her inner self, she stirred up every ounce of strength she possessed to face him.

Queen Zulekha's personal makeup artist had applied her gifted touch to Malika's face after she'd made an earlier appearance as Sule for an hour. Her jaw had dropped when she'd been allowed to look in the mirror. She'd hardly recognized herself through the mask of foundation that matched her dark-cinnamon-hued skin and heavy eye shadow done in shades of shimmery copper and beige. A light layer of false eyelashes swept over her cheeks when she closed her eyes.

Sule had disappeared under the glued-on, curly human front-laced wig that fell to her shoulders, reminding her of the hair she'd cut off in order to play her masculine role. Whoever met her tonight would only see an average height, slim woman wearing glasses. Since the non-prescription accessory had worked for Clark Kent, she had nothing to lose.

With a step forward out of the alcove, she sealed her fate. Air got sucked in as a triple shudder when Zareb's dark eyes met and captured hers. Was it interest or suspicion that kept him staring?

She rubbed her arms to dispel the goosebumps that peppered her skin. In the two-inch heels, she put a bit more swing into her hips as she walked across the floor. Every step jarred her muscles, but it was worth it to see his eyes roam over her from head to toe.

Standing before the duo, her heart skipping a beat when Zareb grinned. In the three weeks they'd been training, his lips had never curved upward in such an obvious manner. A subtle smirk had been all she'd witnessed.

"Where have you been?" The queen didn't allow an answer before saying, "This is my youngest son, Prince Zareb."

Queen Zulekha seemed to take delight in the drama of the moment because the pause was long enough to have had a drumroll.

"My dear boy, this is Malika Ahvanti of Loras."

Malika curtsied as the unswerving attention of Zareb's gaze burned into her.

Rather than the arrogant nod Sule had received, he extended his hand. She reached to shake it, and when their skin met, a current of electricity shot along her palm, shocking her into pulling away. Well, she would've if he hadn't held it hostage.

"It's a pleasure to meet you."

His voice dropped into a smoother, deeper baritone than she'd ever heard before.

She held her body still as a shiver ran along her spine. Her lids slid closed to savour the warmth settling low in her belly. Looking back into his eyes, she tried half-heartedly to extract herself from his grip, but he maintained the contact.

"You also, Your Highness."

The throng of people disappeared as he studied her.

"You're Sule's older sister."

Glad that he hadn't pegged her as Sule himself, she tipped her head.

"My son is chief of security," the queen intruded on the exclusivity they'd been bubbled in. "He does a background check on everyone who resides in the palace. I'm sure he could order Sule's preferred toothpaste if he had a mind to."

Malika giggled, hoping it sounded real. She hated being thrown off-balance, and this situation was akin to walking on a piece of elevated dental floss in stilettoes while tipsy.

Zareb released her hand, leaving her chilled and wanting to snuggle up to his heat.

She watched his hair in fascination as he flipped it out of his face. Unlike when they trained, his glorious mane was free, reaching just below the tops of his broad shoulders. She balled her fingers into fists to keep from reaching out to flaunt decorum and satisfy the desire to touch.

His top, made out of quality yellow brocade, was adorned by black stitching at the neckline that descended to what she knew to be a rippled abdomen. She swallowed the saliva threatening to dribble from the side of her mouth at the memory of his shirtless body, sweaty with straining muscles as he'd pushed himself as if he were the one in training during their workouts.

Malika couldn't pinpoint it, but something changed in his demeanour as he watched her. Unnerved, she'd rather run a mile barefoot over sharp rocks than be intimidated. She maintained steady eye contact with his mesmerizing sable-brown eyes. No hardship on her part as she fell into their depths.

"You hold an uncanny resemblance to your brother."

Taking a risk, she did something that Sule would never do and gave him a lopsided grin as she dipped her chin with a scrunch of her nose. "Yes, we get that a lot. He's told me more than once how much he can't wait for that to change."

As if the three feet between them was too great a distance to be apart, he took a step closer. Her own heeled feet urged her to decrease the gap. She tore her gaze from his by turning her head and caught sight of the queen observing them with a smirk in place.

Malika's cheeks flamed at the I-told-you-so evident in the queen's expression.

He diverted his attention to his mother and tugged on his top. "Where's Sule?"

Queen Zulekha fielded the answer. "He was here earlier. I told him to go up and rest when he mentioned that he was exhausted. The young man seems dedicated."

Zareb glanced between them, and she suddenly felt exposed. Would he catch their scheme? They were playing a dangerous game with a vicious and intelligent man. The combination made her nervous, yet not enough to back out of being Sule.

"Yes," she said. "My brother told me that he has never been trained so thoroughly. He brags about it just before he drops off to sleep while still on the phone with me."

She and the queen laughed while Zareb's expression remained indifferent.

The older woman flipped a ring-adorned hand towards the door. "I see that my husband has returned. I'm going to join him."

Malika's stomach twisted like the string liquorice she used to tie up before eating. Being alone with Zareb wasn't going to happen. "Of course, Your Majesty. If you will pardon me, I'll be leaving soon. I've had a long day."

"I'm sure you have. My son will escort you to your room for the night when you're ready to retire."

Queen Zulekha left, avoiding any potential disagreement with her order.

Unsure of what to do while in Zareb's presence without a sword between them, Malika said the first thing that came to mind. "Have you eaten?"

His lips lifted into a partial smile, causing her heart to summersault. If he would stop doing that, perhaps she'd be able to think more clearly.

"Why do women always seem to care about what's in my stomach?"

"You know what they say about the stomach being the way to a man's heart."

He placed one of his large hands on his abdomen. "Not mine."

"What's the way to your heart?"

She squeezed the metal rim of her clutch bag to stop her throbbing hand from reaching out to smooth his furrowed brow. Strangers didn't caress each other, no matter how much she wondered about how soft his skin would be.

"I don't know. I've never thought about it. It's a good question, though." His gaze arced around the room before returning to her. "I have a question of my own for you."

Whatever he had on his enigmatic mind couldn't be good. Escaping would be a wonderful idea at this point, but she couldn't bring herself to move away from his side. Not when he was being friendly and smelled wonderful. Fresh and spicy, like an orange had been marinated with cloves.

The moment their eyes had met tonight, the truth had leapt in her heart. It'd been more than the fancifulness of a young girl all those years ago when she'd made her childish confession to the queen.

She would marry Prince Zareb.

CHAPTER EIGHT

Forced to blink due to the dryness of his eyes from ogling Malika's striking beauty for so long, Zareb resumed the activity when his lids reopened. Definitely not Sule, yet the two could be identical twins if they had been of the same sex. The difference being that Malika was a fully grown, spectacular woman who knew how to speak her mind and smile, while Sule was a quiet and reserved young man.

He didn't know much about Sule. They spent their time together training or discussing fencing techniques. After the disconcerting reaction he'd had to the boy, he avoided making an effort to get to know him. It had worked because whatever had passed between them hadn't resurfaced. He'd stressed himself out over nothing.

Tonight, he'd focus on Malika's almond-shaped eyes fringed with long dark lashes. The artfully applied makeup emphasized her cheekbones and lips that beckoned to nibble. Would she be a good kisser?

He drew back at the inappropriate thought. He'd just met the woman. And somehow, the electrical currents between them felt familiar. Intense, as his heart thumped against his ribs as if wanting to make its presence aware to her.

She intrigued him. Perhaps it was the way she didn't cower in his presence or giggle like some sort of mindless twit.

"I won't promise to answer your question, Your Highness, but you may ask," she said.

Question? He'd forgotten that he'd had one.

From his peripheral vision, he noticed one of the younger women leading an older one in his direction. His radar went off, and rather than stand there as a blatant target for someone trying to hook a prince, he touched Malika's elbow. The same pleasurable singe of heat he'd experienced when they'd shaken hands zipped up his arm.

The magnetic draw of his body to her brought his lips near her ear. The light, sensual musk of her floral scent hit his nostrils, entreating a longing to pull her against him so he could lick her exposed shoulder.

"Your Highness?"

The huskiness in her voice enflamed his sudden desire.

He cleared his throat and his lust.

"One of the women my mother previously attempted to set me up with is on her way over here. I don't feel up to dealing with her tenacious and rather hands-on nature tonight. Can we take our conversation elsewhere?"

The curt nod served as consent. He guided her through the throng of people, stopping to give brief greetings to a few along the way. He stopped to say hello to his second mother.

"This is my mother, Queen Sapphire. Please meet Malika Ahvanti, the sister of the young man that I have been training recently."

Malika curtsied.

"It's lovely to meet you. Sule is a polite young man. And if Zareb is coaching him in fencing, he must be extraordinary."

Malika's smile took up her face. "Thank you, Your Majesty. I'll be sure to relay the message to my father. He'll be very proud."

"As he should be."

Zareb cupped her elbow. "Malika says that she's tired, so I'm going to escort her to her room."

Queen Sapphire's eyes glittered. "Have a good night."

Back on the path to escaping the gathering, they reached the doors which led to the corridors of his family home. He nodded to the guards on the way out as the tension left his shoulders. With reluctance, he released Malika's arm rather than glide his hand along the radiant skin.

They encountered a few latecomers in the hallway as her heels clicked against the marble floor. His customized soft-soled dress shoes allowed no one to be aware of his presence unless he wanted them to.

"I take it you don't like parties."

He took a double look at the woman whose voice reminded him of Sule's. Odd and disconcerting despite how much he enjoyed it tickling his ear when it came from her succulent mouth.

"What makes you say that?"

"You were over three hours late, and despite the excuse of having a stalker, your light shifting from foot to foot revealed that you'd bolt at any moment."

He added observant to the list of things he'd found to like about Malika so far.

"I prefer to be alone. Engaging with people drains me."

She lowered her head and looked up at him. "And yet, you're here with me."

Was she flirting or just stating a fact? Giving in to his insane desire to drag her against his chest and kiss her would likely get him slapped. He ignored doing anything which would bring a rift between their families and clasped his hands behind his back as they roamed through the palace.

With his need to touch her tucked in a safe place, he spoke. "I noticed that you're not a fan of people, either."

"What gave you that impression?"

"Extroverts don't tend to dwell behind potted plants. They mingle."

The laughter was rich and boisterous as she placed a hand over her stomach. "I should be embarrassed about my behaviour. Or at least getting caught at it."

He let the silence linger, giving her the chance to explain.

"I enjoy parties. What I detest is being set up. It's never ended well for me. I prefer organic meets because they're, well, natural. I was trying to find my way out of the situation with a little bit of decorum." Her hands raised with palms up, appearing like surrender. "Looks like it was an abysmal failure."

"Understandable. I know what my mother is capable of, and I walked right into her trap. It's hard not to when she lays them out with such precision."

Malika nodded with vigour. "She's a genius."

"Indeed."

They took a right at the top of a set of stairs and passed a few doors.

"You didn't want to meet me?" The discernible petulance in his voice irritated him. He wasn't as friendly as his brothers, but he was a catch, even when he didn't want to be.

As if realizing that her words had offended, she placed a hand against his upper arm. The heat spread, swirling into his chest and settling beneath his ribs.

"It wasn't personal." She removed her touch, clasping her fingers together. "I have other aspirations than meeting a man at this point. Getting into a relationship isn't a priority."

"What's your objective?"

"To be the best at what I seek to achieve."

"Which is?"

A smirk lit up her face as she looked at him from the corner of her eye. "Would you believe me if I said, with all due humility, that it's to kick ass?"

The unexpected directness induced a chuckle. "I'd believe it."

"What did you want to ask?"

Zareb's mind jostled to think of something plausible because he'd completely forgotten. What was it about her that made him want to draw out all of her secrets and to reveal the softer, kinder parts of him that only those who loved him knew existed?

Less than thirty minutes had passed since his senses had popped to life with the introduction of her presence. Did she feel it? The sensual energy undulated between them, the likes of which he couldn't recall experiencing. Instinct pushed him to discover more about the beguiling woman.

It didn't make sense to like a stranger immediately. Wariness with a distrust of everything and everyone until he could assess them was more his style. Most people never jumped over that threshold. Yet, here he was, wanting to share without her having proven a thing to him.

Lust. A culprit for drawing a man into situations he didn't belong. It had been a long time since he'd let his libido take charge. He'd gained control over his pleasure-seeking member, understanding the dangers it could lead him into. When he engaged with the women who shared his bed, it was with full knowledge that it would lead nowhere.

As much as he wanted Malika, it was more than desire threading under his skin. He liked her. Not knowing much about her didn't deter the feeling, which set him even further off-balance.

He'd heard of men falling in love after meeting a woman for the first time. He'd sneered when his twin brother Zed had told the story of his initial encounter with Rio because such strong emotions didn't seem possible. Not that he was in love with the lovely Malika, but he could envision himself getting there.

So, he scoffed.

***

Malika jumped at his grunted reply to the innocuous question. Perhaps he was as gruff with everyone as he'd been with Sule. It left her stuck between disappointment and feeling better that he didn't hate Sule.

"Have I offended you, Your Highness?"

His head jerked back. "Not at all. I was reacting to something else. I apologize."

Saliva went down the wrong tube, and she coughed, choking.

"Are you okay?"

Stepping away so he couldn't reach out to pound on her back like she'd have done in this situation, she caught her breath. "I'm all right. In a state of shock from your apology. I could do with some water."

He removed a ring of keys from his pocket and slid the one he'd separated into the door on their right. They walked into a simple yet tasteful suite identical to Sule's. He went to the refrigerator, removed a chilled bottle of water, then opened and handed it to her.

The gentle sip turned into a gulp at being alone. The full-sized bed elicited a fantasy of their skin glistening with sweat as they moved in a rhythm that would lead them to exhausted contentment. It wasn't the first time her imagining him playing a featuring naked role brought a flush of heat to her skin that the water wouldn't be able to douse.

"Are you always so forthright?" he asked.

She snapped her attention away from the bed to meet his penetrating eyes. If only he knew where her mind had gone. "Is this about my response to your apology?"

"Amongst other things."

"I like to be direct when I can. As you know, there are times when having tact is a better way to go."

The sudden snarl didn't startle her this time.

"I prefer honesty," she added. "It's easier to keep track of."

Being Sule brought that to the forefront. Lying was not her thing, and there wasn't a day that she didn't wish she could explain everything to him without getting tossed out of his program.

His chuckle vibrated into her chest as if they'd been bound together.

"You're a unique woman, Miss Ahvanti."

His respectful manner of not taking the liberty to call her by her first name delighted her. "Thank you, Your Highness. Please call me Malika."

He ushered her out the door, closing it behind them. "Call me Zareb. I get the sense that we're going to be good friends. If not more."

Heart racing, scalp tingling, and mouth dry despite the water she'd drunk, anything flirtatious that would've popped out of her mouth with any other man flitted from her brain. "Oh."

"Back to my elusive question from the party. I wanted to know why you and your siblings had such similar names."

It definitely hadn't been the question on his mind. The answer was too direct for his deductive brain not to have figured out. At least, he'd asked something that loosened up the knots in her stomach. Subterfuge wasn't her forte. Having to lie to him any more than she already had might tear a hole in her stomach.

"It's all my father's doing. Malikai Ahvanti has an inflated sense of self."

Dark eyes narrowed, making them more forceful. "You speak of your father in such a manner?"

She took no offense at the gruff way he'd spoken. People tended to keep conversations light and gossipy. For her to share something that may be construed as negative towards herself or her family may seem offensive. "I only told you the truth. He's the first to admit it."

"Is this so?"

His scowl relaxed into an expression of neutrality. The one she had thought was especially reserved for when he trained with Sule.

"Yes. All of his children's names are derived from his. There was only so much variation he could come up with."

They strolled down a corridor she'd never been. She bent to smell a dark pink rose in one of the bouquets displayed in an exquisite vase.

Zareb plucked a flower, removed the thorns, and handed it to her.

She opened and closed her mouth at his sweetness. "Thank you."

He inclined his head in response. A few of his locs fell forward. Not thinking, she reached up and smoothed them behind his ear.

Before she could return her hand to her side, he grasped it and tugged her to him. Where she'd wanted to be all night. Her tongue wet her lips in anticipation of meeting his as his head descended.

Sense thumped inside her skull the moment her eyes drifted closed. Heart racing, she forced herself to jump back. Not even her hand was safe wrapped in his, so she snatched it away and clenched it against her chest.

Strangers didn't kiss. Not in her world.

But I've known him for weeks.

As a bold-faced liar who was using him. He didn't know her from any of the prince-crazy women at the party. Did he think she was an easy conquest? He had no idea how much she already liked him It was no excuse to throw herself at him.

The shake of his head deglazed his eyes before he continued walking, leaving her to follow.

She cleared her throat. It took a couple of false starts in order to regain full speaking capability. "My oldest sister is named Malikia, the brother after him is Malikai Jr. Then there's me. My brother Maliq, who we call Sule because he hates his first name, comes next."

The queen had insisted that she use her actual brother's name while working with Zareb. It would be easier to use the identity of someone who existed. Her brother hadn't been happy with the situation, but he'd allowed it to help her. Plus, he liked when she was in his debt. "What about the last sibling?" Zareb prodded.

Was he really interested in such mundane information? She glanced at him to find his attention fixated on her. Her heart fluttered.

"The challenge came when my parents had another boy. Dad named him Maleek, with two 'e's."

"Things must get confusing in your house."

"They do. Sometimes, when my parents stumbled over calling out the right child, my siblings and I used to laugh."

Her mother had been the guiltiest of butchering their names. Oftentimes, she'd go through the list of them before landing on the one she wanted.

Malika tucked her trembling bottom lip between her teeth, wanting her mother back. Yes, she was in a better place where pain could no longer ravage her, but the void she'd left had been filled with a misery Malika couldn't shake.

The past few weeks spent at the palace, staying busy with fencing while maintaining her business and taking an online class as forced onto her by Zareb, had helped divert attention from the long-suffering grief.

71

Yet, the yearning for her mother hadn't been eradicated.

Zareb stopped and faced her. "What's wrong?"

Swallowing a lump in her throat, she fought the oncoming tears. "I miss my mother."

Silence met her admission instead of platitudes about seeing her mom in Heaven one day or something about the pain going away in time.

She stiffened at the tenderness in his hands as he pulled her into his arms. Who was this man who'd been kind and gentle to her all night when he'd shown Sule an aloof professionalism? This newly discovered sympathy had her melting against his broad chest as he caressed her back with slow strokes.

The sadness that had nearly overwhelmed her slowly receded, transitioning into a raw need to be closer to him. Wrapping her arms around his waist, she allowed his strength to seep into her. Her breath flittered out as a contented sigh.

"You got along well with your mother?"

His voice rumbled through his chest into her ear. "Yes."

He squeezed her tighter. This was not the hard coach she'd been trained by over the past few weeks. This man had the ability to show a grieving woman compassion in her time of need.

Malika permitted herself to be held and comforted for a little while. Although resistant to pull away, she forced herself to be strong. Until he knew who she truly was, there could be nothing between them. A relationship based on lies would never work.

And yet, if she didn't prove herself as Olympic material, he wouldn't allow her to train with him as a woman. Her instincts screamed that if she revealed her true identity now, he'd be throwing her out of his gym before she could finish the sentence.

Biding her time would be best. Otherwise, she'd lose Zareb, the Olympics, *and* her heart.

CHAPTER NINE

Zareb hadn't intended to try to kiss her.

If he were strapped to a lie detector, the pen would be zipping up and down the paper. It had been his sole intention to devour her full lips. Lowered eyelids with her angelic face tilted up as she'd inched closer had indicated that she'd wanted the intimacy just as much. Until she'd brought it to a screeching halt.

Malika had more self-control than him. And that was saying a lot considering how much he'd accomplished with his life. Yet with her, he'd been ready to relinquish it for those moments of anticipated bliss.

She wasn't having it, and he didn't blame her. They'd just met. He'd seduced more than his fair share of women on a first date, but he could sense that Malika was different. Her pulling away said as much.

"How long will you be in Bagumi?" he asked.

"I only came for the party. I'll return home tomorrow."

He frowned at the news, hoping to have more time with her. He'd just met the first woman to fascinate him in years, perhaps his entire lifetime.

"Would you consider staying for a few days? Or just tomorrow? I enjoy your company, and I'd like to get to know you better."

The truth sounded a lot like begging, but he didn't care. In the dimmed lighting of the hallway leading to the palace offices she shook her head.

"Zareb, I—"

He pointed to her leg and cut her off the predicted rejection. "I noticed you wincing when we walked up the stairs. Are you okay?"

The way she crinkled her nose as she shrugged was adorable.

"It's no big deal. I overdid it on a workout. It's catching up with me. My personal trainer is a beast."

"Exercising is the best way to get into shape. You can't forget to rest, though. I'll treat you to my recovery mode day tomorrow. How does that sound?"

"What would that entail?" As if realizing something, she waved a dismissive hand. "It doesn't matter. I have pressing issues to attend to tomorrow."

"Are you scheduled to work?"

"I need to get some rest before the workweek begins." Her lips rose into a light smirk. "My boss is tough."

"What do you do?"

She held her purse up in front of her. Like a miniscule shiny shield?

"I own my company. Do you think Sule has a chance of qualifying for the Olympics?"

Such an abrupt manner of changing the subject. A style he didn't appreciate unless he was utilizing it. A heavy discontentment sank into his stomach that she hadn't enjoyed their time together and wanted to get back to hiding from their set-up. He'd oblige.

"Your brother has potential. If he continues to work hard, he may make it." He threw her a warning look before her grin could broaden any wider. "I'm registering him in an annual competition that my gym is holding in three weeks. It's not the biggest tournament he'll enter, but it will allow me to assess his skill level better."

Her brows scrunched together. "He didn't mention a competition."

Zareb reached out and slid his knuckles along her cheek. Her lips parted with a soft gasp. When she placed her hand over his, the air he'd been breathing became lighter, fresher.

Rather than shock her with a kiss filled with the full extent of his unexpected desire, he removed his fingers from her luxurious skin and continued the trek through his home.

It took a few seconds before she moved to catch up, giving him time to recover. He balled his trembling hand into a fist. Getting the chance to touch her had been intoxicating. What would happen with a kiss? He'd probably feel as if he'd stuck a wire hanger into a wall socket. Malika's appeal was potent.

"Sule doesn't know that he's registered for the tournament," he said, glad that his voice remained steady. "I'll inform him during our next training."

He fought the peculiar hesitance that had claimed him. He hardly knew this woman. Her rejection would be meaningless. Yet, the hard beating in his chest said differently.

"Will you come to the competition?"

She tucked the corner of her bottom lip between her teeth and looked to the right. "I—"

"It's a one-day event. There will be people coming in from all over the world. I've organized it for the past two years. The prizes are pretty large for such a small competition. That's what draws the international fencers. And I'm sure Sule would appreciate your support."

If he stopped babbling, he'd seem more like a man in control, rather than a nervous boy trying to chat up an attractive woman. To distract himself from the odd butterflies tickling his stomach, he herded Malika towards her quarters on the guest side of the palace.

"I'm going away in three weeks." She shrugged a slender shoulder. "It's a planned event, and I can't miss it."

The extent of his displeasure didn't sit well. "Do you like fencing?"

Her face seemed to light up. Or perhaps it was just the moonlight streaming through the curtainless row of windows they were passing.

"I find it fascinating," she said.

"Do you fence?"

"I do. I discovered it when Sule came home excited from a school break years ago and used me as a guinea pig to practice. I was hooked. I joined a club while in college."

He decided to do something he'd refused to do since the accusations that could've ruined his life. He'd tried to avoid entanglements with women, and yet, here he was, willing to do anything to be with Malika. A woman who could fence was a rare find. The fact that she was attractive, intelligent, confident, and had been approved by his mother meant that she had to be for him. Self-promises be damned.

"We could spar."

Her brows drew together. "I was told you don't work with women."

That caused him to pause for a beat. "I don't. How did you know that?"

"Um, your mother told me." She wiped a hand down her skirt. "I was curious about who Sule was going to work with."

His mother detested that he'd struck off training women. More times than he could count, she'd tried to convince him of how ridiculous it was to allow one woman's stupidity to ruin it for others. He understood her position and had listened to the lectures with patience. He'd never clarified that it had been more than a singular incident that had driven him to make such a radical decision. He welcomed females in his gym, but the concept of several times bitten, forever shy had stuck.

At least, his mother would never tell her the reasoning behind his decision. The exploit a selfish young woman had placed him in had cast the Saene name under a negative light so she would've kept it hidden.

Tucking his past away, he focused on Malika and grinned in a way that he hoped didn't make him look like the Big Bad Wolf out to get what he wanted. "I wouldn't be training you. I'd be spending time with you under the guise of having a workout."

CHAPTER TEN

A bone-chilling paralysis that reminded Malika of the frigid winters from her days at college in Indiana infused her body. Only this time, it was Zareb's hungry smile and the sudden invitation to fence with her rather than the whipping wind attacking that sent her into a state of shock. Why couldn't this lack of sexism have existed before she'd had to learn how to walk in a masculine manner?

But then again, just because he'd offered to spar with her didn't mean he would've agreed to coach her. It was a line to get to see her. It tickled her insides to know that he liked her.

But it didn't matter. She was in the situation and would stick with it until she could confess her sins. Confused about the turns her life had taken, she knew one thing, for sure. No matter how much she wanted to, accepting his offer was out of the question. Maybe if she didn't respond to his invitation, he'd let it go.

"It's late. I should get to my room. I need to rest."

He considered her with his head tipped forward as he held her gaze before nodding. She couldn't think of anything to say to dispel the discomfort, so the stroll felt like it took a lot longer than it should've.

Malika ran light fingers over the elegant reddish-brown wood door of the room Queen Zulekha had assigned her. "This is where I'm staying."

After she'd removed the key from her clutch purse, he took it and inserted it into the lock, opening the door.

"Thank you," she mumbled.

He moved forward, crowding her space.

"Will you take me up on my offer?"

The hair framing his face created a curtain of privacy leaving only them in the world.

"I didn't think you were serious."

"I'm not the comedic sort."

Boy, did she know it. "Thank you for your generosity, but I have to decline. I'm involved in a project that takes up a large chunk of my time."

Hours of being run into the ground by a sadistic, yet brilliant fencing coach.

And when she wasn't training, resting, and eating healthy, she was working. There was also that mandatory online university course he'd insisted on. She'd chosen a basic IT class that didn't take much of her time or brain power because she'd learned it as an undergraduate.

Zareb had insisted that fencing wouldn't be Sule's only source of knowledge. The man had a scope of thinking that never failed to impress.

He lessened the gap by a step. "I'm not someone who takes no for an answer."

Squaring her shoulders and straightening her spine until the muscles clenched, she glowered up the remaining six inches.

"That sounds a hell of a lot like a bully. I'm not one to be told what to do, Your Highness." She squinted to emphasize that his title meant nothing to her. "By anyone. I appreciate your generosity, but *no*. Thank you."

Reaching out with his right hand, he stroked a finger along the side of her neck. Tingles eased the indignation and annoyance she'd been gripped with. When his lips trailed along the same line, her breath caught. Weak in the knees, she reached out and grabbed his arm to keep herself upright. Solid muscle under her calloused palm thrilled.

All coherent thought disappeared as he pulled back to gaze into her eyes.

"I know you're attracted to me." He squeezed a normally ticklish area of her waist.

She held back the moan that should've been a giggle.

A mental shake cleared away the pervading image of those lips on other places of her body enough to remember her mission in Bagumi. "Once again, I'm sorry, but I think it—"

The words were cut off as his lips claimed hers.

The slow descent of his head had made his intention clear. She'd wanted his kiss too much to stop it. How long had she been hungry for him? Not just tonight. It had been controlled agony watching and wanting but keeping herself in check.

The guilt over the lies she'd told to preserve her training spot with him had no power here. The press of his firm yet soft mouth created a need that took precedence over everything else. Not even her mind had the gall to argue her out of it when the more aroused areas of her body had taken over.

She responded without hesitation by gliding the tip of her tongue against his lower lip. He opened his mouth. Those strong, capable hands gripped her hips. The entry into his warmth left no regrets as she explored. His deep moan caused her core to clench. Every inch of her was on fire.

His tongue swirling with hers reminded her of the sport they both loved. Only no one was trying to win. It was all about pleasure. He definitely knew how to give while she had no difficulty taking. Gripping her arms around his wide shoulders, she clung, bringing her body flush against his as she delved and parried into his mouth. Tasting, teasing, and needing every stroke that they shared.

She tangled her fingers into his locs, pulling him closer and angling her head so she could do a better job of devouring. The intoxicating light musk of his natural scent combined with his spicy citrus cologne had her wanting to climb up the mountain of a man to get closer.

Without warning, she stood devoid of his heat radiating into her. The loss of his touch left her muddled as she closed her mouth, still craving him. She opened her eyes when she heard a male voice say, "Good evening."

The prince, seeming to have recovered, returned the greeting. "Good evening, Osa. How are the rounds going?"

"Fine, Your Highness. Everything is in order."

Zareb dismissed the guard with a nod.

Malika kept her head bowed while footsteps made their way down the hallway. Her skin had yet to cool. Neither from their encounter or the humiliating fact that she'd been on the cusp of getting caught making out with someone Zareb considered to be a stranger.

Never one to run away from a confrontation, Malika raised her eyes only to discover passion swirling in the depths of his. The throbbing at her centre returned. She'd never wanted someone more.

There was only one thing to do. She leapt into his arms and stood on her toes to reacquaint their mouths. The taste of Zareb on her tongue exploded as she took in as much of him as her greed would allow.

Her hands roamed over his back as her breasts pushed against his steel chest. Nobody had the right to be so physically perfect.

A wanton moan of desire registered. When she recognized it as hers, she understood that she'd gone too far. So, what if she'd wanted this for three weeks while he'd only known her for a couple of hours? Throwing herself at the prince was bad decorum.

But it felt so good.

Logic took over, and she tore her mouth away.

He didn't get the hint when he nibbled along her collarbone. Large hands against her ribcage came within an inch of touching her breasts where her nipples strained against her satin bra.

Panting, she placed her hands against his shoulders and gave a slight shove only for her to be the one to step backwards from the immovable man.

It had been the right thing to do as her breaths were no longer filled with him. They were moving too fast. Whatever was going to happen with Zareb, she refused to regret it. If it occurred tonight without him knowing who she was, she'd break that one promise to herself. No matter how much she wanted to give in to her baser, more delicious raunchier urges, she'd force herself to wait until honesty unravelled between them.

He had the right to know.

She hitched her thumb behind her in the last direction she wanted to go. "I'm heading inside. Have a good night. Thank you for walking me to my room."

May you be blessed with more riches and power for giving me the best kisses of my life.

At his step forward, she utilized one of her fencing footwork moves to slide away from his raised arm. The quick movement ensconced her safely inside. It was much easier to do the right thing when he wasn't touching her.

He grinned. "That was a well-executed retreat."

The metal of the door handle bit into her hand. "Thank you."

"I won't disturb you with my offer again this evening. But I'll be in touch."

His husky voice tempted her to invite him into her suite to carry out every one of the erotic fantasies she'd had about him. She closed the door a little in order to protect herself from his domineering presence. "Goodnight."

He didn't have her private unlisted number so she had no concerns about him calling her.

She'd have taken him up on his offer if she felt he would train her as more than someone he wanted to show off to. Yet, he'd never mentioned or boasted about his Olympic medallist status, which would impress anyone.

Zareb stepped back instead of advancing, and the disappointment of having him leave created a hollowness in her chest.

"I'll speak to you soon," he promised.

She held back a sigh.

Sooner than you think.

CHAPTER ELEVEN

This is a training session just like all the others. No need to be nervous.

Malika wished her moist palms would listen to her brain's message. She'd returned to being Sule and had sulked around the palace all day Sunday hoping to catch a glimpse of Zareb. As much time as he spent in the place, he'd only be seen when he wanted to. Or maybe he'd spent the day in his own home miserable because they weren't together. A woman could dream.

Anxiety over seeing him again after tackling him with a kiss had carried her to the gym thirty minutes earlier than their set appointment on Monday. The steel doors of the locked facility pressed into her back as she contemplated how his lips had tantalized her. The way he'd pulled her to him as if he already knew her body sent a shiver rolling down her spine.

"Are you cold?"

Malika jumped to her feet. The man could sneak up on a ghost. "No, Your Highness."

Unlike previous days, this time, his assessing scowl disturbed her. Would he recognize her as Malika? The pain in her stomach had to be an ulcer. Now that he'd met her as Malika, the torment of deceiving him had worsened. He deserved better.

She needed him as her coach, though. Their chemistry had been explosive the other evening. It wasn't until she'd cooled off that she'd spent most of the night researching coach-athlete romantic relationships. She'd read through the 118-page International Olympic Committee Code of Ethics handbook and found nothing that could deter her and Zareb from being together while she trained.

They were both consenting adults. There was no rule against it. Several Olympic participants had been coached by their spouses. Not that she and Zareb were married, but their relationships had to start from somewhere. She had a feeling that he would see it a whole lot differently.

The click of the lock opening was loud in the tomb-like quiet of the early morning.

"We're holding our annual fencing competition here in three weeks," he said once they'd entered.

She could feel his gaze on her in the low-lit gym. Pulling a Zareb, she kept her expression neutral while she waited for him to make his point.

"Are you interested in participating?"

"Yes."

He gave her a hard look. "I thought you might be a little more enthusiastic about it."

Malika hitched a shoulder. Over the past few weeks, she'd enjoyed acting like a teenager. It was more fun the second time around without those unstable hormones controlling her.

Portraying as if she weren't dancing inside, she mumbled, "I'm excited."

A muscle twitched in Zareb's jaw. "Go change."

Why should he care if Sule didn't react? It wasn't as if Zareb emoted well. Until last night when he'd thrown about his smiles as if he were a normally happy and relaxed man, she'd have described him as being made of marble. Gorgeous, but cold.

She bowed her head as she trudged to the locker room. She preferred the Zareb that had made her boil over with desire.

No matter which persona he displayed, she was still anxious. Not just about him discovering her ruse, but about being so close to him. God help her if he decided to go shirtless. He might find himself slapping her hands away from exploring. That would be horrible for her cover.

**

Zareb shook off the sense of foreboding that had enshrouded him as he watched Sule go to the locker room. Uncanny how much the boy resembled his sister. Not to mention uncomfortable. The need he'd had last night to reach out and touch Malika had mimicked itself today as he stood with Sule. He'd had to stop himself from tugging the boy into a hug.

Frustrated after thinking he'd had himself in control when it came to Sule, he stomped through the facility and tossed his gear into his office before getting the gym ready for opening. Something he normally left to his staff, but he'd been restless when he'd awoken earlier than normal.

Women never got into his system so completely that he'd allowed them to consume the thoughts that work tended to occupy. He couldn't stop thinking about the conversation they'd had. Or their kisses.

Other than his usual security rounds, Sunday had been spent hunting for everything about Malika that he could find.

The search he'd initially done had been focused on Sule when he'd arrived. Zareb had found little of interest. The boy had studied in Spain at the brother boarding school that Malika had attended. As Sule had mentioned, he'd competed on the fencing team there.

His sister, on the other hand, had been humble when it came to her fencing career. He'd watched a few of her clips, and she'd been excellent. She and Sule shared a similar style. He'd found a short video that they'd posted of them full-on sparring when she'd gone to visit her brother at school in Barcelona. He hadn't been able to tell who was whom with their masks down, but they'd both been skilful with a similar style.

The duality of pride and disappointment had warred. Why hadn't she told him that she was that good? She'd brought up his not training women. Did she think he'd scoff at her accomplishments because she was a female?

It wasn't out of disrespect for women that he didn't train them. Their treachery could damage without needing a weapon.

Fariah.

The name clawed against his brain. She'd tried to shackle herself to him using blatant lies she'd thought would destroy him.

He tugged his shirt over his head and wiped away the memory of her idiotic viciousness.

His thoughts turned to Malika and how impressed he'd been with her business acumen. His resources had allowed him to dig into the finances of the company she co-owned, Quest Technologies. She and her partner were on their way to becoming top contenders in the industry.

Driven, successful, intelligent, strong, and beautiful. The perfect combination for him.

Right after the workout with Sule, he'd call the number he'd acquired from his background search. He'd impressed himself by not contacting Malika the moment he'd received it on Sunday.

He missed her.

***

Why?

Malika was seconds away from falling to her knees while screaming an elongated version of the word.

What had she done to deserve such punishment? Backing off on the teenage angst attitude was her new order of business if this was the end result. No longer able to support herself on her legs, she slid against the wall to the floor. Unwilling to embarrass herself by curling up into the foetal position and whimpering, she picked up her bottle of water and guzzled the cool drink.

Her mother would've been appalled at her lack of civil behaviour as liquid dribbled down her chin. Malika didn't care. She'd lost enough sweat today to fill a bathtub. She needed to replace the fluids fast now that the threat of vomiting from exertion had retreated.

Their standard five-mile jog had led to sprints. Then, he'd had her hold various fencing stances on a low balance beam for interminable amounts of time. At least, he'd done it right alongside her. After that, they'd gone fifty rounds of fencing bouts. Not once did she strike a point.

She was starting to believe that the one time she'd scored against him had been a fluke. An aberration never to be repeated. Perhaps she wasn't as good a fencer as she'd thought.

Snap out of it. Crawl over to the other side of the room and grab another bottle of water so you can start thinking clearly again.

The concept of moving remained a thought. She couldn't do it. Instead, she willed the water to her with her mind. It stayed on the table since she had yet to master any sort of telekinesis.

Heavy lids drifted closed as her tongue became sandpaper dry.

"Here."

Zareb's baritone startled her. Not enough for her to open her eyes or demonstrate a defensive position. That would be too much work. What could he be offering? More torment?

"Take the water."

It took two tries to reach out her right arm. She gave up and used her non-fencing hand to grab the bottle. When their fingers touched, an electrical current moved through her. The sensation caused her to snap her eyelids open. His face was an expressionless mask. Had he felt it, too? His sudden steps backwards told her he had, but she couldn't be sure.

It hit her that she was supposed to be a guy. The poor man must be freaking out if he was reacting to her in this state the same way as he did Malika. The thought of hurting him upset her.

It would ease his mind if she came clean. She swirled water in her mouth and swallowed, intending to do just that because she didn't want him questioning himself.

"Sentiment will not make you a champion."

The queen had emphasized the statement with a stern glare when she'd presented the idea of her acting like a young man.

"You must do what you have to do. Right now, that's to acquire this masculine identity. Trust me. I know my son."

What had happened to him in order to make him so adverse to working with women? She'd spent hours searching the Internet in an attempt to discover the truth. Other than when he was associated with his family, fencing, and his many endorsements, the man kept his name out of people's mouths.

She couldn't risk letting him learn that it was Malika who sat crumpled in front of him.

He'd just have to live with his reaction to her being a male. She pacified her guilt by reminding herself that it wouldn't hurt him to be off balance for a little while. At least until the competition. If she lived that long.

A small part of her was happy that he'd reacted to her in both forms. After all, she was the same person. His attraction to her was real even though he didn't know the truth. Something else he might not be able to forgive her for.

Would she have the compassion to let the betrayal go if their roles were reversed? She could only pray that he wasn't half as much of a grudge-holder as her.

She gulped down her near-admission with the water.

"I know I worked you hard, but slow down on drinking. I don't need you choking."

She'd roll her eyes at his supposed kindness when she left his sight. Right then, she had to peel herself off of the floor so she could head back to the palace and die in the comfort of her bed.

CHAPTER TWELVE

He was running out of ways to justify his disturbing reactions to Sule, especially since the spark that had passed between them had been reminiscent of what had occurred with Malika each time they'd made contact.

Attraction.

Zareb mentally gripped the word, slammed it down, and stomped on it. That was not a possibility.

Isn't it?

He growled at his mind to keep it quiet.

He wouldn't go there. Ignoring any questions about his sexuality had kept him sane when it came to Sule, so he'd continue with his own rarely administered *ignorance is bliss* protocol. He left the young man to recover from the gruelling workout. Perhaps he'd driven him too far today.

Yet, it had been Sule who'd requested to train with him, not the other way around. The one thing he'd promised himself when he'd retired from competitive fencing was that he'd lead others to their greatness in the sport. Sule had so much potential that he shone with it. Zareb would do everything in his power to make him a champion.

Without a backward glance at his new protégé, he strode to his office to shower. Undergoing the process on autopilot, he contemplated the best encounter he'd had with a woman in a very long time.

What was it about Malika that intrigued him? There was more to their attraction than a beautiful face. Her strength and willingness to reveal it had impressed him to the point of needing to touch her. His skin sizzled thinking about her fingers flexing against his muscles. Those plush lips and tongue had responded in a way that set off a ball of fire low in his belly.

There was more than the physical between them. When was the last time he'd laughed with a woman who wasn't a close friend or family member? That had to mean something.

Maybe for once in his life, he shouldn't attempt to understand and strategize.

Now this woman had him thinking ridiculous things. He'd be going against his nature if he didn't try to figure it out in a logical manner. No. What he needed was to organize a plan to see her again.

By the time he stepped into a pair of khaki trousers, he'd established an idea. Minutes ago, he'd left the closest person in his sphere to Malika lying in a heap on the floor. Using Sule would be easier than asking his mother. He didn't need her bombarding in on his personal business any more than she already did.

Marching out of his office into the main gym, he waved to some of the members without stopping to converse.

He pushed open the door to the men's locker room. "Sule."

No response. He walked into the open area flanked by lockers. The sight of the young man lying on the bench not appearing to be breathing brough him to his knees.

"Sule!" he said louder as he shook his slim shoulders. "Sule, are you okay?"

***

A rough squeeze of her person was followed by yelling in her ear. She swatted the hand away. Why was the voice calling for her brother while shaking her? The insolence.

Malika attempted to escape the rudeness only to find her limbs flailing before being caught. She popped her lids open and met the familiar eyes of the man she'd been dreaming about moments before. The lingering sensual vision of lips and hands gliding over wet places on her body made her face grow hot as she reached out to capture the strong arms holding her.

Eyes hooded, she grasped the muscles and drew herself to him. Her dream man.

Focused on his tempting lips, she was magnetized to the goal of experiencing the pleasure that Zareb had initiated her to.

The cinnamon freshness of his breath fanned her face as the distance closed, not just from her side. She wasn't the only one lost in the sensations swirling between them, which heightened her desire. Heat penetrated into her skin where his powerful hands held her steady and evoked a moan.

The next thing she knew, she was sprawled out on the floor when he released her. Quick reflexes saved her from face-planting and ending up with a broken nose.

Glancing down at her chest to make sure she'd flattened her breasts, she remembered wanting to rest for a minute before heading to the palace. At least, she'd been smart enough to get dressed in her smock first.

Zareb's stony expression no longer revealed the concern she'd glimpsed seconds ago. "Let's go."

He hadn't been able to hide the huskiness in his voice, and her core throbbed at how she'd affected him. They both had issues to deal with. She now understood just how bad his were. Poor man.

The one thing she could ease his mind about, her being a woman, stayed stuck in her throat as she considered her goals over his distress. The selfishness brought on yet another bout of shame to contend with.

Getting to her feet, she avoided his eyes. "Where?"

"To the palace. I'm giving you a ride."

She squinted, attempting to decipher what his ulterior motive could be. He'd never offered anything other than exercises to improve her fencing skills. Wary, she accepted the ride with a curt not.

Heaving her bag over her shoulder, she followed him out. Had he felt her breasts when he'd prevented her from falling? Doubtful since his hands had held her shoulder and hip. Nowhere near her chest.

As she passed the floor-to-ceiling mirror, she ensured that she looked like the male she was supposed to be portraying. She attempted to add an extra bob to her walk, but then decided against it when it took too much energy. Shuffling would do.

The prince tapped his foot as he waited for her to reach the car. She threw her bag into the open hatch door of the large black Range Rover SUV before sliding into the plush leather front passenger seat. She bit her lip to restrain a whimper as she closed her eyes and leaned her head back, luxuriating in how the seat moulded around her.

Sensing him watching her, she turned her head and opened her eyes. The sharp inhale of breath scratched her throat when she met his inquiring gaze.

Coming to her senses, Malika gave her attention to the passenger side window.

Over the soft purr of the engine, Zareb spoke. "Tell me about your sister."

She slanted her eyes at him. The man intended to pump her for information about ... well, herself. Giddiness wiped away her fatigue. On Saturday, he'd shown his interest, but she'd thought it would wane. If hers hadn't, what made her think his would've?

Despite the crappy situation she and the queen had created, it wasn't all bad. She could have some fun with this. "Which one?"

He took a right out of the parking lot. "Malika."

"Oh." She dulled her voice. "You mean the headstrong one."

He cut her a look that would've had her averting her eyes if she weren't so happy. Did he like her enough that he was annoyed by someone calling her names? "Okay, so she's not always stubborn, but she can be a pain sometimes."

His upper lip curled into a semblance of a smile. "I know what it's like."

She sneered. "You have a bossy older sister who likes to tell you what to do all the time and thinks she's always right about everything?"

It made her day to lord it over her younger siblings, and sometimes her older ones. She couldn't help it if nine times out of ten, she was right.

"I have an older half-sister from Queen Sapphire. Isha likes to be in control as much as I do. Let's just say that I understand."

Remembering to bring on the aloofness, Malika ignored him by watching the lush, manicured landscape of the deepening palace grounds. In the mornings, one of the chauffeurs drove her to the gym. If she wanted a ride back, she'd call. Usually, she opted to walk the two miles. It helped to cleanse her thoughts and commune with nature before delving headlong into her job.

Not deterred, he asked, "What does Malika like to do with her free time?"

"You know, *girl* stuff."

"Such as?"

The sprawling fortress appeared up the road. "Shopping, reading, hanging out with her friends."

Zareb smirked. "Guys don't do those things?"

He had her there. Perhaps she should've added painting her fingernails on a daily basis, but that would've been a lie. She'd rather gnaw them off with her teeth. She had better things to do with her time, like enjoying her family.

When the vehicle stopped, she hated having to leave his side.

They got out, and Zareb grabbed her bag from the rear of the car and tossed it to her.

He slowed his pace to match hers. "I can't get over how much you resemble your sister. It's uncanny."

She hunched her shoulders and scratched her nose. "I get that a lot. It's not a compliment from my point of view."

The most confident man she'd ever met opened his mouth then closed it with hesitation. "Does she have an intended?"

The chuckle she couldn't hold back came out as a sputtered cough. "Intended?"

"Is she dating anyone?"

"Not that I know of. I like to stay out of her business. She can get a little, um, harsh when she thinks someone is invading her space."

Malika took a second to observe him. No reaction.

She wondered why he didn't live at the palace, especially since he wasn't married. "Where do you stay?"

"I built my own place about five kilometres from here."

The marble floor gleamed as they walked into the expansive entryway.

She may as well get some answers from him while she had the chance. "Why?"

She waved a hand at the opulent surroundings, from the crystal chandeliers to what appeared to be original works of art from both African and Western artists. Who wouldn't want to live here?

"This place is ..." She held back the ornate words she'd use if she were herself. "Cool. There's always delicious food available, and I never have to clean my room."

He rubbed his chin as if thinking. "I left for freedom and independence."

She'd attended school outside of Loras for the same reasons. Her family was so close that it sometimes suffocated. Now, her heart longed for that nearness, the reason why she couldn't bear to be more than an hour's plane ride away from them again.

"I see."

"Do you?"

"Yes. Sometimes, being around family and people in general gets stifling. Having a man-cave as a home is the way to go."

Zareb graced her with one of his rare smiles. Malika's stomach dipped, and she turned her head so he couldn't see the desire most likely burning in her eyes. It wouldn't do for a young man to get a crush on his male trainer seeing as how homosexuality still wasn't an openly accepted practice in many countries in West Africa. Loras and Bagumi included.

Was Zareb closed-minded when it came to the topic? After those brief encounters they'd had where she'd realized his reaction to Sule, she doubted it. If he were, she had no misgiving that he'd have kicked her out of the program. Which would've been fine because she'd have lost all respect for him.

"I'm heading up to my room. Will you be coaching us this afternoon?"

The later sessions were group-based. Those who had full-time jobs during the day would join them. The workouts were challenging and expansive as she practiced against those who were already on the Bagumi fencing team.

She held her breath, not sure what she wanted the answer to be. If he said yes, she'd suffer. But if he said no, she wouldn't get to spend time with him. Lately, that's all she wanted to do. Get to know him better. Not that he ever allowed it, though, not until he'd met her as Malika the other night.

"No, I won't."

"Oh."

"I thought you'd be happy." His eyes sparkled when she glanced up at him. "You looked like you didn't want to get off the floor at the gym today."

"I'm glad you find that amusing, Your Highness. I learn a lot when you work with me."

He quirked an eyebrow. "You don't benefit from my other coaches?"

Not falling into the trap of judging his staff, she backed up a step. "I do, but I absorb more from you."

When I'm actually paying attention instead of being hypnotized by your melodious voice.

The light patter was Malika's only warning before a toddler came into the hall, giggling as he lunged himself at Zareb.

"I'm going to get you," a non-menacing voice said just before a man appeared around the corner.

The child's squeals got louder as he attempted to hide behind Zareb.

Prince Zediah lurked in the large hallway, twisting his body as if searching. "Where's my son?"

The boy giggled as he clung to the back of his uncle's legs, hiding his face. The child was too cute for words, and the whole scene made Malika smile.

Zareb looked up at her and did a double-take. She sobered, relieved when he reached down to pick up his nephew.

"He's right here." He blew a raspberry onto the toddler's stomach, causing him to squirm and laugh even harder.

Zareb settled the boy on the crook of his arm and pulled a tendril of his hair. The child returned the gesture with a fistful of Zareb's locs.

Malika ducked to hide just how touched she was by the scene.

"The little stinker ran away when I told him it was time to get back to the room for a bath." Zediah poked out a finger to tickle his son.

Feeling more composed, Malika looked up at the three males. Her heart stopped beating when the child reached out for her.

"Tee."

Chapter Thirteen

Malika glanced behind her to ensure that the child wasn't reaching for someone else. She'd encountered him at the palace a few times, but it wasn't until they'd met at the party while she'd been Malika that they'd engaged. The boy had distracted her with joyous play as she'd waited for Zareb's arrival.

Unable to resist Nour's call as he twisted over Zareb's forearm, she grabbed him, making sure to hold him in front of her body like Zareb had, rather than perched on her hip.

Nour clapped his hands against her cheeks. "Tee. Tee. Tee."

Malika prayed this kid wouldn't expose her before she was ready.

"Nour, That's *Uncle* Sule," Zediah introduced them. "He's not an aunty."

"Tee," he insisted.

Zediah shook his head. "He must have you confused with your sister. You look more like twins than Zareb and I."

"I was just telling him the same thing," Zareb said.

"Tee."

She couldn't discern if Nour's intuition told him that Malika and Sule were the same person or if he was as stubborn as his uncle in believing only what he knew to be true.

Zediah laughed as he took the boy.

"Amira has you calling everyone aunty." He tipped his head towards Zareb. "You need to teach him how to say uncle."

Malika looked at Zareb. The usual neutral expression had been replaced with one of curiosity and a concentrated study of her face.

The sooner she left, the less her chances of being discovered, especially with a tattle-tale toddler on the loose.

"Thanks for the ride. I'll see you later." Hefting the strap of her bag onto her shoulder, she dredged up the strength to climb the stairs.

***

Zareb followed his brother into the quarters he shared with his wife. His parents loved having their grandson in Bagumi. Which worked out because Zed and Rio claimed to appreciate the attention the family gave the boy. His brother lived in a wing opposite from everyone else, but it would drive Zareb nuts to be back under the restrictive roof of his parents.

Zed handed his child over to the woman who was more like family than a nanny. Oksana received him with the same broad grin that Nour brought out in everyone.

"Hey, Zareb."

"Hi, Oksana. Are you missing the cold weather yet?"

"Never," she said with a laugh.

He watched them walk down the hallway as Nour chatted her ear off in a language only he understood. He'd never been one to enjoy children, but his energetic nephew had changed his attitude.

Would his child look like himself or the mother?

An image of Malika's sweet face came to mind.

He'd met her once and was thinking about having children with her? Something had to be wrong. Maybe stress had gotten to him and he was losing it.

"Where's Rio?"

Zed hitched a thumb in the direction of the bedrooms. "Resting. I didn't realize that she'd need so much of it once she'd gotten pregnant. I wish I'd been with her when she was carrying Nour."

"Why? So, you could've gotten on her last nerve by coddling her?"

"Exactly. My queen deserves the best."

"I don't doubt it, but you might want to lay off a little. Give her some space."

Zed grunted. "This coming from the most overprotective person in the country."

"I've eased up a little. Or do you want guard detail with you twenty-four-seven again?"

"No, thanks. Want a drink?"

Zareb took a seat. "I'm all right."

"Now tell me about Malika and how she has you strung out over her."

He couldn't hide anything from Zed. "What are you talking about?"

"This, dare I say it, happiness you're enshrouded in." He wiggled a finger around Zareb's face. "Soft eyes. It's the only thing you can't control."

Zareb rested his forearms on his thighs. "You're being ridiculous. I only met her the other night."

Zed shrugged. "Have you been in contact?"

"No."

Silence.

It didn't take long for the confession.

"When I called, I got a message that her phone wasn't in service. I tried to get information from Sule about her." He tamped down the memory of what had happened in the locker room. If he didn't think about it, then it wasn't real, right? "Such an ornery teenager. I didn't get a chance to ask much about Malika."

"Wouldn't want the kid to know you're interested in his sister by asking him straight out."

He ignored the sarcasm. "You know I'm more about covert actions."

Zed chuckled. "We're all aware of how much you enjoy being a sneaky bastard."

No denial necessary. "Looks like I'll have to go to Mama."

His brother sucked air through his teeth, "That's extreme. Can't you do some of the investigating you've been trained for?"

He frowned. "It would take time, and I already have so much on my plate."

"This Malika must be special."

"She is."

Zed clamped a hand against his shoulder. "Then go for it. How about if I intercept by asking Mama for the contact information? She won't harass me."

Zareb knew he should man-up and go to his mother himself, but he'd have to be drunk to make it happen, and he didn't handle his liquor well. "Don't bet on it, but thanks. I'd appreciate it."

"Need any other info on your crush?"

If she'd agree to come back and spend time with me.

The thought excited him. When he'd first seen Malika, the familiarity of having known her all his life had been jarring. She captivated him.

And for some reason, so did Sule. She must've been on his mind when he'd thought Sule was unconscious in the locker room. His eyes had deceived him when they'd been that close, and for those few seconds, he'd have sworn that Malika, rather than Sule, was with him.

He was tempted to tell Zed about what had been going on when it came to Sule. His brother wouldn't judge.

Yet, as comfortable as he felt with his twin, Zed wasn't the confidant to discuss it with. All he'd give him was encouragement to explore. His half-brother Zik would be the one he'd confide in if he ever wanted an opinion. They shared the qualities of being disciplined, honest, and direct, but somehow, Zik had tapped into his emotional and compassionate side without going overboard. Zik gave practical advice that Zareb had taken on more than one occasion.

He sighed and got to his feet, already knowing the outcome on the topic. He wouldn't need to talk to anyone about Sule, because there was nothing to discuss.

CHAPTER FOURTEEN

The musical ringtone pulled Malika out of a zone of concentration she'd spent the whole of Saturday afternoon in. The client would love the work she'd done to make the program both accessible and easy to learn.

When the ringing occurred again, she realized it was Malika's rather than Sule's phone.

Private number showed on the screen. The raised hairs on the back of her neck told her who it was without answering. Should she ignore it? With reluctance, she pressed the answer button and grumbled, "Hello?"

"Malika."

She loved being right. She'd recognize the voice of her prince even if she were underwater, but he didn't need to know that. "Who is this please?"

"Zareb Saene." He paused, seeming to expect her to jump in.

She took pleasure in waiting for him to continue.

"We met at the palace in Bagumi last Saturday evening."

A broad grin accompanied more silence on her end.

"At the party. My mother, Queen Zulekha, introduced us."

"Ah, yes. I remember. One of the princes." It was getting harder to keep from laughing. Only a week had passed since the party. How could he think she wouldn't remember him? "How are you?"

"I'm doing well, and yourself?"

"I'm fine, thank you."

"Will you be attending the fencing tournament to see your brother compete?"

So much for small talk. Why hadn't she chosen any of the more flirtatious princes to become infatuated with? "Nothing has changed. I'm not able to make it."

"Is that so? Can't you rearrange your plans?"

She rubbed a hand over her mouth to wipe the grin away so it wouldn't come through in her voice. "It's something I can't postpone."

Please don't ask what I've got going on. She had a back-up story of being a bridesmaid in a cousin's wedding ready to blurt out, but she'd prefer not to lie. At least not any more than she had already.

"I was hoping to see you there."

"Why? To show off your favourite sport?"

"Partly. I enjoyed our time together. I'd like to get to know you better."

Heat streamed up her neck as she recalled their kisses. "I had a good time, too."

"When will I see you again?"

"I don't know. My life is a little ... complicated right now."

"Tell me about it."

She heard no trace of sarcasm. He really expected her to tell him what was going on. The hard part was that she wanted to get it off her chest. How angry could he get?

A volcano spewing hot lava and destroying everything in its path flashed before her mind's eye. She couldn't risk exposing her secret before he saw her potential as an Olympic hopeful. Or was good and properly in love with her. That would take time, if it ever happened.

"How about ..." she hesitated, pretty sure she was about to do something dumb, but unable to resist temptation. "If we meet for lunch next Sunday?"

She put a pillow over her face and bit down, waiting for her conscience to tell her she'd done the wrong thing.

Nothing came. No sense of impending doom at seeing him again. A lightness made her feel as if she were floating. She'd made the right move to see him again.

"I'd like to, but will it make your life more complicated?"

Without a doubt.

"I could use the diversion."

"I'll see how distracting I can be."

There was that humour he hid so well with Sule. Did she have a right to be jealous of herself?

"I'll take the early morning flight, and we can hang out." She couldn't believe her boldness. "I can only stay for a few hours. I have an appointment at six."

"I could come to you in Loras, if that would be more convenient."

Extending her arm forward, she waved as if he stood before her.

"That's okay." She took in a breath to reduce the shrillness, then rushed to explain the lie. "My meeting is with your mother."

Must remember to call the queen and fill her in.

"She gave me an assignment which I'm on the verge of finalising," she continued. "I need to give her a report before the next phase can begin."

"What's the project?"

"It's still in the works, so I can't discuss it yet."

"Okay, then it's a date. I'll pick you up from the airport next Sunday."

"No!" she shrieked. There had to be a way to respond that didn't make her seem so suspicious. "I mean, that's not necessary. I know you're busy with your work. Your mother said she'd send a car to get me."

Malika released her breath when he didn't contest her statement or try to convince her to change her plans. Whatever happened, she'd have to find herself at the airport looking like a vivacious woman who'd just stepped off the plane, in case Zareb decided to show up.

The queen would have to devise a diversion to keep him from being there on time for the touchdown; otherwise, she'd be toast.

"Do you mind if I call you before then?"

He was asking her permission? *Wow*.

"That would be fine."

"Good. What do you have going on for the day?"

Opening her mouth to speak, nothing came out. With every turn, he surprised her. She'd never have guessed that he'd care about her mundane plans.

"Hello, Malika. Are you still there?"

"Yes. I was going to call my brother to check up on him. He always seems so tired. What have you been doing to him?"

"Making him earn my mother's interference into my training centre."

Her shoulders drooped. "Are you punishing him?"

"Not at all. I'm whipping Sule into shape. He's talented, and I want to draw it out so that he has no doubts."

She snorted. "Believe me, Sule is aware of his gift in fencing. Training, winning competitions, and going to the Olympics is all he talks about. He's lucky to have you as a coach." She paused. "Thank you for taking him on."

"After he got in a hit during our interview session, I had no choice."

She knew better. No one forced Zareb to do anything he didn't want to do. Not even his mother. Time to change the subject. "What are you up to today?"

"Working. Because of this tournament, we need to vet everyone who will be coming."

"Sounds like a good time."

He chuckled.

"It's what I live for."

She gulped, hoping he didn't look too much deeper into her or Sule. She'd had to do a search of everything that she'd ever posted on the Internet and get rid of the things that might've made her look like a liar. Being deceptive was exhausting.

"What do you do for fun?" she asked.

"What's fun?"

Was he serious?

"I'm kidding. Exercise of any form is my greatest enjoyment. Being with my family and the few friends that I've been able to maintain over the years.

Watching movies and reading is one of my favourite pastimes, although I don't make much time for it. What about you?"

He had her at reading. "Pretty much the same, only I have loads of friends that I like to talk to and hang out with."

"I can understand why. You're pleasant to be around, and I can't wait to spend time with you."

His honesty was pure charm. "Thank you."

"I'll let you get back to your day."

Don't go yet. "Yeah. I'm sure you're busy."

"You sound disappointed."

May as well be upfront. "I'm enjoying talking to you. You're different from what I thought you'd be."

She could get used to that deep-chested laugh of his.

"I'm almost afraid to ask. In what way?"

"You have the reputation of being a disciplined man who endures no nonsense. When your mother said she wanted to introduce us, I didn't expect you to be so ... well, nice."

"Don't let anyone outside of my family hear you say that. They'd never believe you. I'm not an easy person to get to know unless I open up, which is rare."

She touched the base of her throat to find her pulse throbbing. "And you're willing to open up to me?"

"Very much so."

The guilt of her lies piled higher with a force that made her slither onto the floor wishing she could confess.

A muffled knock sounded from his end. "I could talk to you all day, but I have a meeting."

"Okay. That's fine."

I'll spend my time daydreaming about you and wondering why you like me when all I've done is deceive you. No big deal.

"Have a good day, Malika."

"The same to you, Zareb."

When the phone went dead, she stared at it for the longest time. Had she really just arranged a date with the one man she should be staying away from?

Yes, indeed. And she was going to keep it. Like her mother had once told her, things always worked out the way they were supposed to. There was no time like the present to believe her.

Malika peeled herself off of the floor. She had a date to plan for. It was a week away, but preparations had to be made if she wasn't going to get caught in the process.

She'd packed a suitcase full of her Malika clothes. One of the outfits would do. She looked forward to wearing something sleeveless to show off her toned arms, and wouldn't mind revealing a little bit of cleavage, either. Not that she had much to flaunt, but her hyper-padded push-up bra would provide her with what nature hadn't.

First things first. Call Queen Zulekha.

CHAPTER FIFTEEN

Zareb swung into the first parking space he saw and jumped out of the vehicle, hoping he hadn't missed Malika's arrival. His mother had been so demanding with her requests that he couldn't have escaped without completing them. No one was rude to the queen without severe consequences.

Malika had told him not to come, but he couldn't have stayed away if he'd actually put effort into it. They'd conversed every day for the past week, and he couldn't wait to be with her again.

Dashing into the airport, he scanned the area. He froze, mesmerized as he caught sight of her. Rich umber skin glowed as if she'd ingested a star. Glorious. She'd worn a traditional bright multi-coloured print cloth sewn into a modern wrap-style dress which showed off her trim figure. She'd changed her hairstyle and now wore braids which hung to below her shoulders. A different pair of glasses than she'd worn at the party adorned her face.

Stepping forward, he fell into her view. He could tell when she recognized him by the initial broad smile which she immediately converted into a frown. Her glittering eyes presented the truth. Watching her stalk in his direction, he'd never seen a more striking woman in his life.

She curtsied when she stood a few feet away. The respect ended there as she placed a fist on her hip. "You don't follow orders very well, do you, Your Highness?"

"Only when they make sense." Giving no heed to protocol or the people present, he closed the space between them and embraced her.

His body stirred when she wound her arms around his neck and squeezed. How could he have missed a woman he'd known for a week?

Because we belong together.

As the thought crashed into his consciousness, he released her. When she clung, he tightened his arms again, not caring if anyone was minding their business. He'd kiss her if Bagumi didn't possess a conservative culture when it came to displaying affection.

On his second attempt to let her go, she loosened her hold.

Clearing his throat before speaking didn't remove the huskiness when he asked, "How was the flight?"

She blinked a few times. "Uneventful."

He doubted that a day trip would require more than a carry-on, but couldn't assume that she'd come without any bags. "Do you have luggage?"

"No."

They walked to the parking area in silence.

Unlocking his SUV with the key fob, he settled her in the passenger seat before jogging to the driver's side to bask in her euphoria-inducing presence. He was a goner. Settled, he angled himself to better stare into her luminous dark brown eyes. "I'm glad you're here."

"I—"

He cut her off by leaning in and brushing his mouth against hers, then nipped the bottom lip lightly with his teeth. When she responded by placing her palm against his cheek while sealing their mouths together, he hauled her over the console to sit across his lap as he deepened the kiss with a sweep of his tongue into her warmth.

He tightened his grip on her hip when her moan vibrated into his chest. Her tongue sliding against his in such earnest had him ready to crawl into the backseat with her. Always advancing, never retreating, she gave so much of herself. Engulfed in the flames she'd sparked, he lost all sense of place and time as being with her became the only thing that mattered.

Zareb raised his head and sucked in air to replenish his lungs. The tinted windows were lightly fogged. How long had he been in paradise?

Not long enough. He lifted her onto the passenger's seat with a whimper of resistance on her part.

Turning on the engine, he rolled down the automatic windows to let the slight breeze in. Not that he minded being immersed in her lilac scent, but he needed the windows to clear so he could drive.

Hands busy straightening her dress, she kept her gaze on her lap.

Would she chastise him for doing what they'd both obviously wanted?

"I thought I told you not to pick me up."

He'd hoped Malika wasn't one to dwell on a subject. At least, this topic was easier to handle than discussing the explosive attraction that had his fingers wrapped tight around the steering wheel to stop himself from touching her. Pulling out of the parking lot, he contemplated how to answer. Not that she'd asked a question, but the accusation was clear. At the red light a few meters away, he turned to look into her face. Stunning.

"I missed you and wanted more time together. Is that all right?"

Just like his hug in the airport, his confession seemed to take the temper out of her.

"Oh."

"I won't share you with your brother. Not today. You can visit him another time."

She looked down at her lap. "Sule said he'd be sleeping and studying, so he'll be cool with me not visiting."

"He'd better be," he mumbled to himself.

"What was that?"

"I said that I was glad to hear that he'd be okay about you not seeing him."

She snickered, but said nothing.

A mile of road passed before he spoke again.

"I know you wanted to meet for lunch, but it's only ten in the morning. I thought I could take you back to my place. We can relax with a movie of your choice, have lunch, then continue with more films."

"I hope you're not thinking I'm a Netflix and chill type of woman. Because I'm not." She crossed her arms over her chest. "Just because we kissed doesn't mean it's going any further."

He fought his cheeks to hold back a grin. Her honesty had to be the sexiest thing about her.

"I meant it about just hanging out. Talking. Getting to know each other."

"Oh."

He arched a brow. "I wouldn't be averse to taking things further, if you insist. We're both mature adults who know what we want. When you're ready, I am."

The light changed, and he drove as his offer hung in the air. Just when he thought she'd ignore it, she shook her head.

"I'm not ..." She gulped. "Us kissing the night of the party and at the airport was—"

"Phenomenal."

The corner of her lip disappeared between her teeth.

"Yes. But what I'm trying to say is that it's not me. I'm a slow mover when it comes to getting to know a guy."

And yet, she'd dived right in with him. Vulnerability on his part might put her at ease.

"If it helps, when the number I had for you wouldn't go through, I sent my twin to my mother to get your contact information."

"Why didn't you go to her yourself?"

He held her gaze for as long as the stretch of road would allow. "I didn't want to hear her gloating about being right. She's really good at it."

Malika's laughter brought on his own grin.

"I wish I'd gone to her, though," he admitted.

"Why?"

"I would've enjoyed hearing the story about how when you were seven, you announced to my mother that you were going to marry me."

She smacked both palms over her face. "Oh, my goodness!"

He reached out and tugged at her hand. When she relaxed, he interlaced their fingers. He'd have no difficulty getting accustomed to the electricity that sprang into him.

"Do you remember making the declaration?"

"That was a long time ago. The musings of a small girl crushing on someone who was kind to her."

At least, she didn't deny it. "Looks like we've known each other for eighteen years, Malika. Kisses between old friends is nothing to feel bad about. I'm not a stranger to you."

"Did you remember me?"

Smart woman. "No, but you were familiar."

She shifted to look out her side window, the reflection of the glass revealing a grimace.

"What's wrong?"

"Nothing. I've had a demanding week. I wouldn't mind relaxing and watching movies for the day." Long-lashed eyes squinted. "That's all."

"We can sit in the most public place of the palace if it's what you desire, just as long as I'm with you. Nothing will happen that you don't want."

"Why doesn't that sound comforting?"

He held up his right hand. "I'm a man of my word. No one in Bagumi would refute it. What I say is the absolute truth."

"I believe you."

"Good."

She angled her upper body towards him. "Now for the hard part."

"What's that?"

"What movie are we going to watch?"

A rough guffaw scraped out of his throat. Malika had a way of entertaining his spirit.

"Since you'll be a guest in my home, we can watch whatever you choose."

"An artistic foreign film with subtitles."

He winced. "If that's what you want, then sure. Don't be surprised if I engage you in a lot of conversation throughout."

Her giggle was the second best sound he'd heard from her. The moans while they'd kissed were number one.

"I can't say that I'd mind," she said.

Glass-fronted-storeyed buildings reflected the sun on the horizon as they got onto the highway. "The next time you're in Bagumi, we'll go into the capital city. Have you ever been there?"

She hinged forward as she took in the skyline. "No, but I've seen it every time I've flown into Bagumi. I'm sure the pictures on the Internet don't do it justice. From this view, it looks spectacular."

Proud of his country and his family's accomplishments with the land, he nodded. "They don't call it the pride of West Africa for nothing. I'm looking forward to your return so we can explore."

He got the sense that no matter how often they met up, it wouldn't be enough. For now, he'd enjoy her willingness to share her time with him.

***

Zareb parked in front of a two-storey house settled within a copse of trees. What had she been thinking when she'd agreed to come to his home?

After a month of training with him, she'd concluded that he was a good man. Disciplined and respectful to everyone she'd seen him come into contact with, even though he was a prince.

His invite had been to watch movies and eat lunch, so she was sure that's what they'd do.

Then why was her skin feeling clammy and her hands trembling?

It wasn't Zareb she didn't trust. She desperately wanted a repeat of the groping session they'd had at the airport. If it had been up to her, they'd still be in the parking lot, possibly getting arrested for indecent exposure.

The trip out had been filled with light conversations about whatever came to mind. He was an easy man to be with. If the time they'd already spent together was any indication, it would mean she'd made the right decision to see him again despite the further lies she'd had to tell to make it happen.

She assessed how his house was camouflaged to fit into the nature surrounding it as they got out of the car and walked to his home.

"Do you live here by yourself?" she asked as he unlocked the door.

"Mostly. Occasionally, my brother Zik drops by when he needs some privacy."

"I've heard about Zik. Isn't he the one the media labels as a playboy? Does he bring women here to have sex?"

Where was her filter? Gone with her nerves.

His bark of laughter amused her as they stepped into his home. "I'm not at liberty to say."

"Hmm. What about you?"

The hold he held on her gaze made her lightheaded.

"I don't think you really want to know." He swept a hand towards the interior. "Please, come in. It isn't anything like the palace, but it's home."

Gulping down a repeat of the question he hadn't answered, she decided that not knowing was best. His inner sanctum would reveal who he truly was. Give her some insight into more of his personality.

She learned nothing on the tour. The place consisted of dark wood furnishings and lacked any hue that wasn't brown or a variation of it. She hadn't expected his home to be decorated like a rainbow, but some colour, even if it consisted of orange throw pillows on the couch, would make the room pop a little.

Was this his personality? Non-dimensional? If she'd only known him as Sule, she'd think so, but she'd seen deeper into him. During their conversations, he'd not only been thoughtful, but thought-provoking. He'd brought up world topics that had them arguing at times, agreeing at others. His sense of humour often surprised her. He was also caring—she'd witnessed it in how he treated his family, especially Nour.

The friendliness and passion he'd shared made her wonder where the vibrant reds and purples were in his world. The brilliant fireworks of colour that he caused her to see with his heady kisses should be splattered all over.

"Have a seat," Zareb offered. "What would you like to drink?"

"Water."

She watched his well-built frame as he left the room.

Malika's gaze drifted to and lingered on the unique carvings of the furniture which gave the place a traditional appeal. The abstract art he'd hung neglected to add hominess to the eggshell-shaded walls. She shouldn't be surprised since he probably spent more time protecting the palace than he did in his home.

It didn't take Zareb long to return and hand her a chilled bottle of water before sitting on the couch at a respectable yet still too close a distance. "These paintings are astonishing. Are you an art buff?"

"It was my minor in college. My father passed on his love of art."

If only she hadn't become enraptured with every new thing she learned about him. The tenderness in his eyes when he'd mentioned his dad spoke volumes.

He reached out and grazed the back of his fingers over the crest of her cheek. She dipped her head closer, silently asking for more. She would've never guessed him to be a person to display his affections so readily.

Ask the queen how he is with other women.

Her mouth went into an automatic purse at the thought of him being with anyone else.

"Does my touch annoy you?"

She crinkled her eyebrows together. "No. Why do you ask?"

"The tightness of your mouth. You seem upset. I was wondering if it was because I'd taken the opportunity to touch you."

She summoned the courage to ask the question plaguing her.

"Are you like this with all of your partners? I mean." She slapped a hand against her chest. "Not that I'm yours or anything. I was just wondering," she mumbled.

Her orator ancestors would disown her for the inarticulation.

She'd maintained eye contact the whole embarrassing time, but the gleam in his eyes made the situation worse.

"I don't tend to be an affectionate person. You and my nephew bring it out of me."

Mouth suddenly dry, she reached for her water, untwisted the top, and took a drink. "What are we going to watch?"

"It's your choice."

A man true to his word. Another tick in the positive potential boyfriend column. Who was she kidding? In the short time she'd known him, he'd already filled in every space of several Bingo cards of what she liked in a man.

Now to see how he'd react to her choice. She'd spent a significant amount of time trying to decide on a movie that wouldn't make her squirm with explicit love scenes, but that they'd both enjoy. She'd taken it as a personal test to see if she knew him at all.

"I choose *Hotel Rwanda*."

He angled his head to the side. "Interesting. I've heard of it, but never seen it."

"Me neither. I hazarded a guess that you like documentaries, and this is based on a true story."

"What made you think that about me?"

"You're practical and down to Earth. Someone who is always learning."

Those beautiful teeth of his flashed.

"Although true, I also enjoy the chance to escape when I find the time to read or watch movies. Action, adventure, fantasy. If it's a good enough trailer, then a romantic comedy." He shook his head. "But nothing sad, depressing, or political. Life is full of that already."

Not what she'd expected. "So, what are we going to watch?"

"Do you like romance?" he said in a lowered voice.

Her stomach flipped at the caress of the words. "It's okay. Better in real life than in movies."

"Are you a romantic?"

"I'd like to think so. You?"

He stood. "I'll be right back."

Gone for less than a minute, he returned with his hands behind his back.

She watched with a thrill of curiosity as he presented her with a gold box from his right hand. Her mouth dropped open.

"This is the perfume I've been wearing lately. How did you know?"

He tapped his nose. "I have three sisters and two mothers who have exquisite taste. I insist on being the one to escort them when they go shopping. I wasn't exactly sure if it was the kind you wore, but I knew you smelled like lilacs with a light fruity undertone."

The toughest man in Bagumi was melting her heart with his observational sweetness. "Thank you."

His other hand presented her with a second gift. This one was wrapped. She guessed that the flat parcel was a book as she looked up at him before receiving it.

She opened it and gasped. A sketch of her from the night they'd met at the party sat in a gilded frame. "This is beautiful."

"I drew it from memory."

The pads of her fingers brushed against the delicate strokes used to replicate her exact likeness. "Oh, my goodness."

He shrugged. "Zed is the artist in the family, but I have skills too. I just don't make money from them like he does."

Her chest tightened, and she gulped to maintain control of her emotions.

"Thank you, Zareb. And yes, you are."

"What?"

Their gazes linked. "A romantic."

"Now you know."

CHAPTER SIXTEEN

It would be impolite, not to mention illegal, to strip the lock from his door to keep Malika with him for the determinable future.

The movie *Hotel Rwanda* had ignited bouts of outrage at the injustices by and against humanity. They'd also discussed the goodness that people could display when they chose to.

After devouring the lunch he'd had a palace chef prepare and deliver to them, they'd settled in for an action-adventure of her choosing. Twenty minutes into the film, Malika's head flopped onto his shoulder. He'd looked down to find her eyes closed and her breathing deep and rhythmic. Adjusting their bodies, he'd looped his arm around her so that his chest became her pillow.

He was in heaven with her snuggled into his side. How had he gotten to this point so fast? Deep down, he knew she was the one for him. Why would she have such a captivating and soothing effect if she wasn't?

He switched off the movie, grabbed his tablet, and assessed the camera feed at the palace. For the next two hours, he sent instructions to his second-in-command before researching the remainder of the people who had accepted to attend the competition next Saturday. No participant, coach, or invited guest would enter if they hadn't been vetted. He wasn't taking any chances. If it were up to him, he'd cancel the tournament, but the king and crown prince had insisted on showing the world that Bagumi held no fear.

Zawadi was leading diplomatic talks between the countries. So far, General Noda seemed appeased although the Barakat president was known to be temperamental and could change his mind on a whim.

Zareb's instincts still tingled, but he hadn't pinpointed why. He'd rather play things safe when it came to his family.

Malika wiggled and placed a hand on his chest. The movement was accompanied by a whimper that had the most sensitive part of his body twitching.

Her small palm roamed over his muscles. Without warning, she stopped her groping and went stiff. She shot her upper body away from him and across to the opposite side of the couch. Wild eyes glanced around the room as she placed a hand on her hair and patted it. Recognition seemed to settle when she touched her fingers to the base of her slender throat.

"I'm sorry, Zareb. I didn't mean to fall asleep on you."

"You must've needed the rest."

She nodded. "What time is it?"

"Three o'clock."

"I was out for two hours?"

He crossed his arms to keep from reaching over to draw her back to him. "Yes. The explosions and gunfire in the movie were like a lullaby. You're a very deep and still sleeper."

"I've been told. My sister insists on putting a mirror under my nose to make sure I'm still alive."

That reminded him of the time he'd discovered Sule sound asleep and difficult to wake up in the locker room. It had scared the hell out of him. It must've been what had accounted for his reaction to the young man afterwards. Fear made a person react in odd ways.

Malika stood and grabbed her purse. "I'm going to use the restroom."

She didn't wait for him to speak before pivoting and going. As he watched her, he found a familiarity in the straightforward sway-less stride that reminded him of her brother. If her fuller hips and perfect butt weren't emphasized by the cinched waist of her dress, he'd think they were the same person walking away.

The family resemblances were disturbing. He distracted himself by setting up the movie to the point where Malika had fallen asleep.

She made a quick return, lipstick refreshed.

"Would you like something to eat or drink?"

She sat and rubbed her flat stomach. "All of that incredible food you fed me was probably why I fell asleep. I'm still full."

Holding up the remote control to keep his vision from lingering over her body, he asked, "Ready to continue where you left off?"

"Do you mind if we talk?"

The tight clasp of fingers and slightly higher pitch of her voice didn't intimate that she had a topic in mind that he'd enjoy.

He rested an ankle over his knee and draped an arm over the back of the seat, feigning an appearance of relaxation. "Not at all."

The inward roll of her lips dragged his gaze to a mouth he desperately wanted to taste again.

"Why don't you train women to fence?" She slanted her eyes at him as her nostrils flared. "Do you think we're inferior to men?"

Her hands rose to a defensive position at his bark of laughter. Malika had made him laugh more in the time he'd known her than he had all of last month.

"After meeting my mother, how could you ask such a question?"

Her slim shoulders relaxed. "It's the society we find ourselves. For men, women are to be controlled, not respected."

"Not in my world."

"And yet, your father has two wives. How is this fair to the women?"

Rubbing his chin, Zareb thought about how much to reveal.

"I'm sorry," she said. "I shouldn't have brought it up. It's none of my business." She glanced at her watch. "We have a few hours before I need to be at the palace. We can get back to our movie viewing. I promise to stay awake."

"My mother granted my father permission to take a second wife."

She waved her hands between them. "It's okay, you don't have to tell me."

He felt compelled to confide in her. "I want to. You see, my parents' marriage was arranged. They share a mutual respect, and as much as I hate to admit it, an attraction for each other. Although my father is fond of her, he's with her for political reasons. My mother has loved him since they first met."

Zareb shrugged. "Not long after they were married, my father fell in love with the woman who is now his second wife, but wouldn't act on it out of deference to my mother and her powerful war-mongering family. She had no wish to keep him away from his desire. She didn't want to divorce him, either. As a couple, they were good together. She insisted that she bear the heir to the throne before he took his second wife."

He tapped his temple. "My mother has an analytical mind. Her advice to my father over the years had proven invaluable and profitable. Both had gained from the relationship."

Her braids slid over her shoulder as she tilted her head. "It's sad that it wasn't a love match."

"My mother explained that she'd fallen in love with four of the most beautiful creatures she could have ever created. She would always be grateful to her husband."

"That was sweet of her to allow him to marry."

"You can think that until you hear the other condition she set." He faked a shiver. "I still find this disturbing because they're my parents, but my mother is open with us about everything."

"My mom was like that, too. She expected full disclosure just because she gave it."

"Exactly. Anyway, she told the king that he must continue to be true to her by way of their marriage bed."

Her eyes grew wide. "That might be too much information for me."

This conversation was another way he knew that Malika was someone special in his life. He'd never think of telling his family's secrets to someone he didn't intrinsically sense would keep the information to herself.

"I've always held your mother in high esteem, but she's gone up a hundred more rungs. If she doesn't take care, she'll get to Heaven with the angels."

He chuckled. "Just think of how pushy she can be. That should demote her quickly enough."

"Will do. Now will you answer my question about why you don't coach women?"

If he could reveal private things about his family, he could divulge his own secret. First, he needed something in return.

CHAPTER SEVENTEEN

Her prince had a gift for more than fencing and protection. Zareb had left her vocal cords unable to function when he'd shared a confidence.

Queen Zulekha had confided in her best friend years ago. Malika had heard the story from her mother after receiving her first heartbreak. It hadn't made her feel better that a queen had romantic problems, too, but it had put relationships into perspective. The lesson she'd taken away was that no matter their rank or their upbringing, men were selfish asses who never truly loved anyone but themselves.

It had been a simplistic conclusion, but no man she'd gotten involved with had proven her wrong.

Would Zareb finally be the exception? Things were looking good, but so had all the other relationships she'd been in. At least in the beginning. Maybe he was like his father with a roaming eye. Something she'd never be able to tolerate. She didn't care if he was a royal and this culture allowed multiple marriages. Like her parents' relationship—either she'd be the only one for him, or she wouldn't be with him at all.

She brought her thoughts to a wall-slamming stop. They weren't even together, and she was thinking about binding him to her side. That was crazy. She was no longer a seven-year-old girl with a crush on someone who'd been kind to her.

As a grown woman, she had to choose wisely in order to protect her heart from being obliterated. Yet again.

"Why didn't you tell me that you're involved in fencing and that you used to compete and win at a collegiate level at Notre Dame?" Zareb asked.

Well, damn.

Turnabout was fair play, and her politically-savvy father had taught her how to rotate a situation to suit her.

She added an edge to her tone. "I told you that I used to fence. Why were you in my personal business, Your Highness? You could've just asked me. It would've been the more respectful thing to do rather than digging into my digital life."

The open-mouthed, wide-eyed look of shock did not suit him. "You knew?"

"Of course. As you've discovered, I own an IT company that provides customized spyware for my clients. I got the alert as soon as you started using your advanced system. We do exceptional work at Quest Technologies. You may want to look into hiring us."

Malika took advantage of his speechlessness to keep him on the defensive.

"Not mentioning my fencing skills weren't a big deal to me." She arched a singular filled-in eyebrow in challenge. "It's part of the past, not the present."

If there was a Hell, that's definitely where she'd be heading with all of her lies.

As if catching on to her tactic, his stone face returned as he crossed his arms over his chest. "Then there's no reason to know why I don't train women. Something happened in the *past* to drive my decision. Let's keep it at that."

That hadn't gone as planned. She doubted that anything with him ever would.

"I didn't want you to look at me differently. Your reputation preceded you about not dealing with women when it came to fencing, and I thought you might shut me out if you knew."

Silence lingered to the point of discomfort before he spoke. "I understand, but there were several opportunities to tell me once you realized that I liked you."

Her heart fluttered as his honest charm sent heat creeping up her neck, bringing on a flush to her face. "There was no way to know for sure that you liked me."

Zareb rolled his eyes. "Our kisses and me wanting to spend time with you didn't give you a clue?"

Her cheeks ached from trying to hold back a smile. "Maybe a tiny bit, but I couldn't be certain you wouldn't turn on me. Men can be fickle sometimes."

"Just men? Don't take offence, but in my opinion, women are ungrateful, trouble-making liars who are out for themselves."

"How can I possibly take offence?"

"Not all women are like that. I'd never put my mothers, sisters, or sister-in-law in that category."

That didn't help. Who didn't love their family and try to see the best in them? Even the horrible ones. "What happened to have you despise us?"

The cold-eyed stare indicated that she wouldn't get a full answer.

"Experience is the best teacher."

How she'd love to hear that story. Maybe one day when he was ready to share. "What about me?"

"To be honest, there's something I feel that you're hiding."

The dryness of her mouth made it difficult to speak.

"You're right. I haven't revealed a lot of things about myself." She held up two fingers, waving them in his face. "This is the second time we've met as adults. Am I supposed to bare my soul?"

Tilting his head, he regarded her. "You just went on the offensive for the second time today. My gut is never wrong. You're hiding something. Something big."

Now would be the best time to come clean. She'd yell it to any character in a movie she was watching. But this was real life. Her future was a stake. Telling him the truth before proving herself at the competition wouldn't do her any good. Afterwards, she'd reveal everything.

In the meantime, a limited honesty would have to serve. "I'm not ready to share yet, but when I am, I hope you'll understand."

A few of his locs bobbed forward with his nod. "I can't promise that I will, but I'll listen."

That didn't ease her stress levels, but at least, it wasn't a straight-out no. Just the kind of authentic man he'd proven himself to be. She sank deeper into the trenches of guilt. Why did he have to be so good?

In an attempt to drive the topic away from herself, she asked, "What do treacherous women have to do with not training females in fencing?"

His eyes bore into hers as if he had the power to read her mind. To her credit, she held his gaze without flinching.

"I haven't had the best relationships with women in the past. The one that I'd fallen in love with ended up cheating on me with one of my teammates."

She rubbed her hands over the goosebumps that had erupted from the cold harshness of his tone.

"It was probably my fault for focusing so much on fencing rather than giving her the attention she wanted. Turns out I wasn't enough for her."

Malika's fist balled.

"That's nonsense." She may be biased, but she knew without a doubt that he was more than enough for any woman. "Did you cheat on her?"

"No."

"Then no matter how the relationship was going, she should've communicated it with you." She sucked her teeth. Having experienced infidelity by an ex more than once and having come out the other side more jaded about relationships, she'd learned one lesson. "It wasn't your fault. You're worthy of someone who can appreciate you for who you are."

And she did. Everything about him intrigued her, and she looked forward to learning more. One woman's loss was her gain.

His smile was slight but present. "Thank you."

She cleared her throat, not having meant to come off so passionate about the topic. "I hope she didn't have the power to give all women a bad name."

"It wasn't just her. When I used to work with them—"

She pointed a finger with a sharp gasp. "You coached females? In fencing?"

"I don't know what you've heard about me, but I'm not sexist or a male chauvinist. My mother would've punished it out of me by now. I believe in the equality of men and women."

Other than his one rule, nothing she'd experienced when they'd been together had made her think otherwise.

"Many of the females who worked with me took more advantage of the opportunity to go after me than to develop in the sport with the invaluable fencing lessons I provided. When I didn't reciprocate, they left."

The false lashes she'd pasted on obscured her vision when she narrowed her eyes. "Putting aside having experienced the fickleness of a deceptive ex, that doesn't sound like enough reason to stop training women altogether, especially since it sounds like you may have had some good ones. Did something happen?"

He scrubbed a hand over his face and released a long sigh. "One of them accused me of raping her. She'd been manipulated by her mother to trap me so they could become part of the royal family."

Her head jerked back as she gasped. "What?"

His mouth tightened into a line as his locs scraped his shoulder with his head shake. "It wasn't the first time a woman had attempted to capture me through nefarious means, and I was tired of it. And women in general. Both in and out of fencing. It didn't take long before the truth came out that she'd lied, but by then, I was fed up."

She leaned her upper body back to get a better look at him. "Oh, my goodness, that was you?"

"You heard about it?"

"Who didn't? An adult prince accused of raping a sixteen-year-old is a big deal. They never mentioned which one of you was involved. I always thought it might've been Prince Zik. He's known for his more rakish ways."

The Royal House of Saene was a powerful entity of wealth and influence. If they wanted a controversy to disappear, they had the means to make it so. It was probably why no names had been mentioned when the travesty had happened.

The topic had trended for a day. Then there'd been no further mention of the incident after the announcement that the accuser had lied about her involvement with a prince.

Mouth set in a grim scowl, he nodded once. "My family dealt with the situation and my accuser swiftly and thoroughly."

"What was the punishment? Did you have her executed?"

"No. Not that it wasn't suggested by my mother. She spent time in juvenile prison for the false accusation."

Malika chewed the inside of her cheek while she contemplated how she'd ask the question she desperately needed an answer to. "Zareb?"

"Yes?"

Determined not to back down, she squared her shoulders and held his gaze, needing to know the truth from his own mouth. "What happened?"

His back straightened even further than his impeccable posture normally allowed. "Do you think I raped her?"

She flinched at his bluntness.

"You're known as a virtuous man. Disciplined to the point of android levels, and protective of those you care about."

Now came the part that may sever their burgeoning friendship. "With that said, it never happened to me, but I've heard stories from friends who have been attacked or manipulated by supposedly reputable, decent men. They never suffered the consequences of their horrific actions. The experiences made me furious at the impotence and pain the young women had faced. Of not being believed when they reported to a higher authority."

She huffed out a breath into the tense silence. "It's why I asked for your side of the story. With everything you have going for you, you're still a man. Men are capable of destroying just as much as they are of building."

His Adam's apple bobbed with a heavy swallow. "You're a remarkable woman, Malika. If you had experienced abuse at the hands of anyone, I'd hunt them down and do damage."

How did someone respond to such a statement? "Okay?"

"I'm impressed that you don't believe my innocence just because you know me. No one is ever aware about what a person is capable of until it happens. Keep your pessimistic insights about life, and doubt everything and everyone. It will serve you well."

It didn't sound like the most pleasant description of her, but he'd spoken with pride.

Zareb shifted forward and rested his elbows on his thighs. "As you mentioned, in many cultures, the older members prey on the young and vulnerable, especially the females just because they can. Child marriages have been abolished in Bagumi for many years and is punishable, but it still goes on in other areas of the continent." Those intense eyes met hers again. "I'm not one of those people."

From everything she'd learned, his nature was of stern kindness. It was the way he dealt with Sule. With respect, even though the boy held no ranking or status. Could he hurt another person? Definitely. It was his job to protect. A man like Zareb would take all necessary means to ensure that his people remained safe.

"I used to go to the local secondary school to give demonstrations in fencing," he continued. "I wanted to introduce as many people into the sport as I could. Possibly find the next Olympic contenders from Bagumi. I'd then invite those who were interested to take lessons at the gym for free. I even threw in transportation.

"The boys would flock in, but the girls wouldn't attend. I had a few women learning the sport, but they weren't aspirants. They'd utilize it for exercise. Others had been there to garner male attention. Including mine."

"Which you never gave."

He snickered. "Correct. So, they dwindled out."

"Are you telling me that not one female found fencing fascinating and tried to excel at it?"

"There were a few who had trained hard. Eventually, they ended up having to deal with other responsibilities and stopped attending. It was always a disappointment to see them go."

The muscle under his eye twitched. "Fariah was a different story. I was so pleased about her enthusiasm and ability to pick up the skills that I trained her myself. She had the potential to be great. Until things changed. She started dumbing down her skills and tried to interact with me in a flirtatious manner." His lids closed as he shook his head. "Such a disappointment."

"Did you try to talk to her about it?"

"I sat her down in my office to have a discussion. I have no idea what possessed her, but she stripped off the dress she'd been wearing after practice to reveal her nakedness and then tried to kiss me."

Her mouth dropped.

"I'm versed in self-defence, but hitting a female who isn't armed, and isn't physically trying to inflict injury, is beyond me. I gripped her shoulders and pushed her away, telling her to put her clothes on. I then stormed out of my office to give her privacy and get my anger under control. When she came out dishevelled, she was crying and hysterical. I tried to talk to her, but she ran off screaming that she hated me."

Malika hissed in air through her teeth. "Not good."

"No, it wasn't. Things spiralled from there. She told her family that I'd raped her in my office. They came to the palace the next morning and insisted on seeing the king. In their threat, they claimed that they hadn't mentioned my name to the media they'd already contacted, but they would destroy me and the palace if I didn't marry their daughter."

Hands fisted in fury over the injustice, she shook her head. "They didn't report you to the police?"

He let out a short chortle. "They'd manipulated it. Fariah's mother had coached the girl, setting her up as a pawn to capture a prince. If my name had been attached, the reputation that I've kept unblemished all of my life would've been obliterated, even though I was exonerated."

"Have you always had cameras in your office?"

Stern eyes flicked in her direction. "How do you know?"

"Um. Well. Sule mentioned it." She plucked at her skirt. "If he doesn't make it in fencing, I told him that he should become a police detective. He notices everything. Anyway, back to the story."

The interrogative glower he rained on her made her skin prickle.

"The video vindicated me."

Malika fell back against the couch with relief that he'd believed her. "Good."

"My family is powerful, but people have long memories, especially those who prefer to believe rumours rather than fact. I refuse to bring shame to the Saene name. From that point on, I decided not to train women personally, although they're welcome in my facility."

She didn't completely understand. The saying about throwing the baby out with the bathwater came to mind. He'd lumped all women in a singular group and flung them out of his sphere. But then again, other than by her siblings when they'd been younger, she'd never been accused of doing something she hadn't. For such a righteous individual, it had to sting.

"Then why did you offer to fence with me?"

A smile appeared as he rubbed his chin. "I had an ulterior motive."

Her stomach flipped in the most delicious manner. "Which was?"

"To impress you. Get you to like me."

The flirtation was making her lightheaded. "What made you think I wasn't already impressed?"

His gaze dropped to her lips, but he didn't move. Remembering his promise of not touching her, she took the initiative and scooted over, closing the space between them.

Those all-observing eyes rose to meet hers. "Are you?"

Temptation motivating her, she braced her hands on his cheeks and brought her lips within an inch of his. "Very much."

CHAPTER EIGHTEEN

If Zareb moved, it would be towards the woman filling his sight as her luxurious scent wafted into his nose. He wouldn't allow himself to break his promise, so he held every muscle rigid.

His desire rose with each second that their breaths mingled. She leaned in and grazed her petal-soft lips against his. Their electric touch opened up a need that he'd held banked. He waited to make sure it wasn't a simple kiss.

When her mouth started moving against his, he gave himself permission to indulge in her. He teased her lips with his tongue. When she opened, he entered. Warmth suffused into him as the unique taste of Malika coated his tastebuds.

The uninhibited passion in her response was unmistakable as she explored his mouth. How could each kiss be better than the last? He wouldn't be the one to initiate an end. There was no strength in him to make such an impossibility happen.

When she swung a leg over his and straddled his lap. The skirt of her dress exposed smooth thighs as she lowered herself in a way that left no question about what she wanted. She ground herself against the erection which had refused to die completely down since he'd kissed her at the airport. She pulled away and placed her hands against his shoulders.

Perky breasts beckoned to be tasted as she rotated her hips against him. He bent his head, found the peak, and suckled her through the cotton. She held his head in place as his hand slid up her ribcage and squeezed her other breast.

"Zareb," she whimpered. "More."

The tugging at the tie to her outfit emphasized her need. Then she grabbed the hem of her dress and jerked it up over supple thighs. He released her for the time it took to reveal the muscular flesh of her stomach as she flung the garment over her shoulder.

The light blue lace bra exposed the nipples he'd been indulging in. He palmed the perfect orbs while looking into the dark brown eyes which held fire within their depths.

She unhooked her bra, letting the straps fall while he sat in wonderment at the woman who held more control over him than he'd ever given anyone.

"Make love to me," she said in a strong voice that held confidence. No hesitation.

He responded to the raw need that they shared by capturing her lips in a kiss that made him harder as his hands grasped her bottom and squeezed.

***

As Malika became wetter with desire, so did her need to be filled. Things couldn't have gone any other way. His hardness encased in his trousers rubbing against her core wasn't enough, so she'd asked for what she wanted.

Consequences would come later. Desperate pleasure was for the moment.

Their lips separated with a smack as he ended the kiss and pulled off his shirt. For the first time in a month, she allowed herself to touch the spectacular bare chest that had teased her during their training. Her eyes and sensitized fingers caressed his broad shoulders, glided down his flesh-covered steel arms, and skittered along his ripped abdomen.

His stomach quivered as he gasped in a breath.

He arched his hips, bringing her into more intimate contact with his glorious bulge, hitting her in just the right spot to make her call on her maker. Without warning, she was airborne as his powerful legs pushed them off the couch. She wrapped her limbs around him in wonderment at his strength.

The walk to his bedroom was short as she kissed his neck on every spot she could reach before settling on the area that had made him stop and rest a palm against the wall.

In his bedroom, he didn't lay her on the bed as expected. He opened a drawer, pulled something out, and then left.

Sharp disappointment struck her in the chest. Didn't he want to have sex?

"Where are we going?"

"To the couch. I'm sure that I unwittingly bought it with you in mind."

When he settled her on her feet, he gave her a quick kiss before undoing his belt, the button of his trousers, and the zipper. The apparel hit the floor with a pair of black boxer briefs that didn't keep her interest. The slightly curved erection bobbing up to touch his stomach had more of an impact.

Her tongue moistened her lips as she watched him open a condom and slide it on.

Her hard, fast heartrate strummed in her wet core.

Zareb sat on the couch. "If you want to shift those panties to the side while you slide me inside of you, I'll be okay with that."

Her channel wept and pulsed as the words mimicked something that Zareb in her vivid fantasies would say. Yes, she'd been the one to initiate, but he certainly had no difficulty picking up the baton and running with it.

She hooked a finger inside the lace at her crotch and pulled it over, exposing herself. His gaze never left her as he clenched his fingers on his thighs. Not ready to release the sexual power she loved claiming, she let the moist patch of cloth fall back into place.

Her hands had a mind of their own as she stroked them over her breasts and shook her shoulders to make the small mounds jiggle for him. His hardness bobbed in response to the way she wiggled her hips in a slow manner, as if dancing just as she'd done in her mind for him so many times.

She lowered the ice-blue lace of her panties with the slowness of molasses. When they reached her knees, she let gravity take over before stepping out of them. Every inch of her was hot and ready as she strode to within his touching range.

Zareb didn't move.

He'd given her full control over this experience. In a state of awe, she widened her legs, her intimate scent reaching her nose as she placed her knees on either side of his thighs.

Before she could reach for that impressive member to ease down on, he slid a finger between her folds and caressed until her eyes crossed. Her limbs quivered as his wicked tongue encircled the dark peak of her breast.

"I need you," she panted.

"Then have me, Malika. I'm all yours."

Her lids rose to meet the passionate flare in his gaze.

Capturing his lips with her mouth, she reached between them, grasped his hardness, and brought it to her centre.

She released her mouth from the kiss and grabbed his shoulders as she slid herself down on him. Unhurried, she experienced every section of her channel being expanded. The moans of pleasure were silenced when he was completely inside of her. She could no longer breathe. She'd desired him for the past month, and now, they'd merged.

After taking a moment to adjust to his length and girth, she squeezed her inner muscles.

He let out a roar. "Dear God!"

Drunk with power, she rose until his tip met her entrance. She took the lead of their dance as she alternated between an up and down motion and swirling her hips against him.

He joined in with an upward thrust. Their skin glistened with a sheen of sweat as they retreated and met over and over again.

Knowing what she needed, his finger teased her clit. He applied the right amount of pressure to detonate her over the edge into a release that had her seeing both stars and rainbows behind her lids.

"Yes, Zareb!"

He thrust into her several times before he released an animalistic growl as his body stiffened with his climax.

Time passed with them collapsed and entangled.

Zareb rubbed her back. The gentleness brought on a burn behind her lids.

When she sniffled, he smoothed his hands over her shoulders and looked up into her eyes.

"Are you okay? Why are you crying?"

"I'm great." She grazed a hand along his cheek. "I'm a little overwhelmed with how ..." She had difficulty articulating the experience. "Beautiful that was. How wonderful you are."

He turned his head and kissed her palm. Yet another sweetness she'd hold in her heart forever. There was a lot to learn about the prince.

"Would you like to take a shower with me?"

She reached up and touched her wig with both hands. It had miraculously stayed on. That was some powerful hair glue she'd used.

"I can't get my hair wet."

Not uncommon for a Black woman to say. Although if she snatched the wig off, she could transport them into the shower fantasy she'd been holding onto after a steamy book she'd once read.

"Then we'll take a bath together. Is that acceptable?"

Her imagination went rampant at what could happen. When she nodded, he kissed her lips, stood, and swung her legs around so he cradled her.

She rested her head against his shoulder "I can walk, you know."

"I wouldn't doubt if you could carry me," he teased. "But please, let me spoil you."

She had no will to decline such a generous offer from the man of her childhood and adult dreams.

CHAPTER NINETEEN

"Are you ready for the competition next Saturday?"

Queen Zulekha drew Malika away from thoughts of plotting a time when she could be alone with Zareb again. It was inappropriate on her part to think about how the woman's son had filled and moved within her until she'd exploded with their passion. Twice.

Zareb had placed a chaste peck on her cheek before leaving her at his mother's door at the palace. She'd never known there was such a thing as missing a person when you had been with him only seconds earlier.

"Yes, Your Majesty. I've been able to best quite a few of the men and women I've trained with. I think I'll do well. Your son will finally see that I'm worthy of being coached as a woman."

The queen's head tilted, and her salt and pepper locs cascaded over her shoulder as she seemed to consider her. Zareb was so much like his mother that Malika marvelled at the resemblance.

"From his lovesick expression at having to drop you off, I'm sure he thinks you worthy of other things, too."

She ducked as heat filled her face.

"I know I've told you this before, but your mother was closer than a sister to me, and I consider you to be one of my daughters. No one can replace the wonderful woman who did a spectacular job of raising you, but I hope that you can see me as a surrogate when you need to talk."

The queen had just presented a much less invasive invitation than her mother would've. Malika's ego swelled at the fact that the woman saw her as mature enough to either accept or decline her as a confidant.

"Zareb told me why he doesn't coach women."

Queen Zulekha sighed. "It was a tumultuous time for him. Despite how gruff he presents himself, my youngest son is the most sensitive of all the king's children. He hides it well. His instincts border on clairvoyant at times, so when this incident happened and he hadn't seen it coming, he lost hope. Not just in women, but himself."

Her heart clenched. Here she was doing the same thing to him. Would her deception make him doubt himself again? It was already happening with his reaction to Sule. What had she gotten herself into?

The queen took a sip of the guava drink that Malika had gulped down and hadn't been ashamed to ask for more of. Making love with a man with limitless energy had dehydrated her.

"It happened two years ago, but the damage remains." The older woman flexed and unflexed her fingers as if squeezing something. Perhaps Fariah's imaginary neck?

Malika wanted to do the same.

Hypocrite.

"With you to train, my son is returning to his former self," the queen said. "Has he told you why he'd never returned to competitive fencing?"

Malika scooted to the edge of her seat and leaned forward. "He didn't."

There had been no announcement of him not returning to fencing—he had simply disappeared from the circuit.

"After his bronze medal win in the 2016 Olympics, Zareb was determined to win gold in 2020. He pushed himself hard and injured his hamstring. Instead of resting for the allotted amount of time, he competed in a tournament and injured it further." Queen Zulekha sighed. "I love my son, but three months of recovery with limited physical outlet had not been good for him or the palace."

She could imagine.

"Just as he'd healed enough to return to training, the king had a heart attack. For a while, we didn't know if my husband would survive. It devastated us all."

Malika had heard about the tragedy. Her family had held the king in their thoughts and prayers. "But then, he pulled through and recovered."

The queen smiled. "Yes, he did, with time. It was during that period that our head of security decided to move to the US to be with his family. He didn't want to die without spending time with the ones he loved. Zareb had been his second-in-command. It suited him because he could focus on training while working at the palace."

She made silent guess as to how it all went down. "Zareb took the position. But I don't understand why he couldn't continue with fencing."

"My son's favourite saying is, 'You can't serve two masters.'"

Malika nodded. "He tells me that all the time when he's referring to me committing to a move."

"Zareb fell in love with fencing before he completely understood what it would take to fulfil his goal of becoming head of palace security. When his father sent him off to Royal Military Academy, Sandhurst at eighteen to become an officer, Zareb gladly went. When he joined the army full-time, he did it with pride. It wasn't until he failed to come anywhere near to being a qualifier for the Olympics during that time that reality hit."

Understanding dawned.

"When the 2012 Olympics came and went without him being a competitor, he made a decision and a deal with his father to focus on bringing a medal to Bagumi while learning the ins and outs of palace security as an apprentice of sorts. It all worked out well."

"Until King Ibrahim's heart attack."

"Yes. As a dutiful son, Zareb honoured his father's request without question. He also gave up any chance of going to the Olympics again."

Malika rested her back against the seat as memories of every day she'd trained with Zareb scrolled through her mind. "It's why he's so hard on Sule."

"Precisely. He recognizes your talent and is trying to nourish it. It is my hope that he will remember this when he discovers that you are Sule. That his desire to coach you to a state of greatness will circumvent being ..." she paused for a moment. "Influenced into training you."

"I feel wretched about lying to him."

"I know, dear. You're forthright. Just like my son. But sometimes, a little lie is necessary to reach an objective."

Considering how he sometimes reacted to Sule, Malika couldn't see how it would turn out any way but badly. "He hates deception."

"Yes, but he likes you. He'll get over it."

His mother knew him on a deeper level than she did.

"I wanted you to know his story so that when the truth comes to light and his ire rises, you won't give up on him."

Malika's head snapped back. "I'm sure it'll be the other way around, and he'll never want to see me again."

The queen clasped elegant fingers on her lap. "Be ready for the fallout, but don't lose hope. Everything will work itself out. Promise me one thing."

She hesitated for moment. Deals made with queens rarely ended up well for the other party in fairy tales. This was real life, and Queen Zulekha would never hurt her.

"No matter what happens with him, you won't give up on fulfilling your dream."

Since she'd already made the promise to her mother, it wouldn't be difficult to accomplish her goal of becoming a champion. "I will, Your Majesty."

The newly developed heart-stirring aspiration that saw Zareb in her life for the long haul might not be as easy to attain, though.

CHAPTER TWENTY

Malika's mask echoed with the double-tap Zareb gave it.

"Get your head into the match, Sule. Where's your attention this evening?"

She'd been fantasizing about having more incredible sex with him instead of attacking and defending to win.

"Sorry," she mumbled.

His severe scowl would've had her knees trembling if she didn't know what a sweet, caring, gentle man he could be.

"Focus."

"Yes, Your Highness."

Returning to the *en garde* position, she scrutinized her opponent. A man at least a foot taller than her who knew how to use his height to his advantage. He had the tendency to force his way into her strike zone before she had the chance to parry.

Determined to win, she gave her full attention to the match instead of recalling Zareb's large hands caressing sensitized areas of her skin.

When the referee signalled for them to begin, she didn't wait for her opponent's attack. Two leaps forward and she lunged low, hitting him in the thigh with her sword. The buzzer registered the score.

By the close of the practice session, she'd ended up winning that match along with two more in their round robin.

Another week of practice, and she'd have the first prize from the tournament cinched. That very same day, she'd finally take the opportunity to do what her guilt-ridden mind had wanted to do from the start. Her chest tightened in at the thought of Zareb's reaction to her true identity.

Would his new-found affection for her allow him to forgive the duplicity like the queen was confident of? Would he want to be with her anymore? The last question had her breaking out into a cold sweat.

A hand smacked her on the back, sending her flying a few steps. She turned to glare at the offender.

The prince stood tall and proud with his arms crossed over his chest. "Good recovery after those first couple of bouts."

Malika kept quiet.

"You need to do better." He held up a finger. "From the start, you must be fully in the fight. You won't have another chance if you're eliminated from the first round."

She nodded while restricting her eyes from drifting down to those full, firm lips of his.

"Get your things." His order wasn't as gruff as normal. "I'll give you a ride home."

Malika blinked up at him. First, he showed up to an evening session with a positive attitude, and now, he was being kind to Sule? The man needed to get sexed on the regular. But only with her.

"Hurry up."

In an effort to avoid the men in varying stages of undress, in the evenings, she kept her bag out in the main training area rather than the locker room. She met Zareb waiting at the front desk speaking with one of the gym's managers.

"Let's go," he said once he'd finished the conversation. On the way to the car, he stared at her profile. "You and your sister look so much alike. Like you could pass for the same person with some tweaks."

She'd never understand how she'd choked on air, but it happened to the point of her coughing so hard that she thought an organ would fly out.

"Are you okay?"

Malika held up a hand as she caught her breath. "Yeah."

He knew. Such an observant man had to, right? She was a good actress, but to deceive him to such an extent was Oscar-worthy. Was he playing with her? Luring her into a false sense of security? Maybe he'd expose her in public at the competition as a sham before sending her packing.

Or maybe the queen was right. "The things we want to see, we see."

Zareb needed to train a champion. She'd been hand-delivered to him. He just needed to relinquish his self-imposed rule and allow himself to coach her as a woman.

He clicked the doors open, and they settled into the vehicle.

She'd presume he wasn't up to a grandiose scheme to humiliate her. He was too direct. If he'd discovered her ruse, he'd have said something. Her guilt-reddened conscience needed to calm down.

"I'm not sure if you're aware," she said, her voice coming out steady. "But you keep mentioning our similarity." Malika rubbed her non-existent beard with her thumb and forefinger and tried to broaden her shoulders. "Except, I'm manlier than her."

His smirk hurt her a little as she took it as an attack on her acting.

"What?"

"Your sister is feminine, but I wouldn't call you more manly. You've got to get a voice change and grow some facial hair for that to happen. You need more muscle." He drove out of the space. "In fact, I'm surprised our workout sessions haven't helped you to create more mass."

Malika took offense.

"I've expanded." She drove up the arm of the hand-woven smock and flexed.

For the first time while being Sule, Zareb threw back his head and laughed. It was at her expense, but it heated her like alcohol landing in an empty stomach. She pretended to remain indignant with a huff as she tugged the sleeve back down.

"Yes, you're so buff, you'd dominate in the Mr Universe competition."

Crossing her arms over her flattened chest, she couldn't wait to remove the binding when she got home. She'd never again take for granted a regular bra. "I'm wiry."

"Yes, you are. It helps with your speed, but you could still do with more muscle."

If she were a man, he'd be right. But as a woman, she was as buff as she was going to get without weight training every minute of the day or taking steroids. Time to change the subject to see if she could embarrass him a little.

"Malika texted that she hung out with you yesterday." She glared at him in what she hoped was a threatening manner. "What are your intentions towards my sister?"

Zareb removed his gaze from the road and put her in his sights. "Excuse me?"

"Man to man. What do you have planned? I won't have you using her."

It was good to be a reckless teenager. The repercussion that would come when she exposed herself lay too far away to be considered now.

"That's none of your business."

"She's my sister. I have to watch out for her."

Another hearty chuckle.

This time, she became annoyed. "What's so funny?"

"You've met your sister?" He didn't let her answer. "Is she the sort of woman who needs protecting? In my estimation, she can defend herself and everyone in her vicinity. She's tough."

Malika sat up straight. He'd said it as if he respected the quality. And her.

"Yeah, she is," she agreed with a shocked murmur. "What do you have planned for her?"

"Nothing but good things, Sule. She's an incredible woman who deserves the best."

She hid the irrepressible grin behind her hand as she gave a curt nod.

"Cool. It's been a while since she's had someone in her life. She seems happier these days."

"How long has it been?"

She shrugged. "I don't know. We don't get into it like that. And it would be better if *you* found out from her."

He pulled up to the palace and put the car in park. She stripped off her seatbelt.

"Hey, Sule."

Before she could pull on the door handle, he touched her arm. A familiar tinge of current sprang into her.

Zareb pulled his hand away and clenched his fist. The light from the palace grounds revealed his sharp features inches away. Dark eyes focused on her as he spoke.

"As long as you concentrate at the tournament, I have a feeling that you'll be a contender for the quarter-finals, maybe higher."

He didn't need to reassure her, yet he had. The fact that he'd never shown this side of himself to Sule before made the moment special. A gush of emotion seized her as she realized that she loved him.

On instinct, she leaned forward and kissed his lips. Time froze for a fraction of a second before she found herself shoved away from that colossal mistake.

Zareb swiped a hand across his mouth. If they were outside, she wouldn't doubt that he'd spit.

"What the hell do you think you're doing?"

The bass of his booming voice released the paralysis she'd been stuck in.

In that singular moment, she'd lost her mind. "I'm sorry."

She tumbled out of the open door with the bag she'd held on her lap during the ride. Keeping her head bowed, she turned and ran. Too bad it couldn't be towards the past to redo what had happened.

CHAPTER TWENTY-ONE

The tyres grated against the asphalt as Zareb sped away from the front of the palace and skid around the corner to the parking area in the back. He screeched to a stop in the first space he found and gripped the steering wheel.

The deep breaths he dragged in didn't calm his jangled nerves.

Sule had kissed him, and he couldn't say that he hadn't liked it. That had been the most alarming aspect. The familiarity of those lips had held him still for a second too long.

Heart racing to the point of him feeling lightheaded, he risked getting out and to his feet. The cool night air helped, but there was only one thing he needed.

Running to the door, he flashed his badge at the security scanner and tore through the halls the same way he and his siblings used to run from each other while playing tag on the rainy days of his youth. He held up a hand of reassurance to the guard making his rounds.

Reaching his destination, he smacked the door so hard that it rattled. Past experience had taught him that using his key to enter his brother's suite tended to make him a witness to things he should never see, so he held back.

Shuffling his feet, this time, the base of his fist hit the solid wood.

When the barrier swung open, he passed by his older brother. Whipping around, he announced, "I need to talk to you."

Zik rushed up to him, concern etched into his pinched features.

"What's wrong? Is everyone all right?" He placed a hand over his chest. "Did Baba have another heart attack?"

A clear sense of perspective returned as he realized that things could be worse. A lot worse.

"Everyone is fine," he said in a calmer voice. "I have a personal issue."

Zik glanced over his right then left shoulder to find the room empty. "Zed isn't here."

"I came to talk to you."

"Me?"

Any other time, he would've been amused by his brother's reaction. To be fair, he rarely took his problems to anyone, not even his twin. His way was to come up with the solution on his own since he knew himself best.

Zik headed to his minibar. "Want a drink?"

"Scotch. Straight."

His brother dropped the glass he'd been holding. Luckily, it hit the counter of the bar and didn't shatter. Zik raced over to him.

"Zareb, are you dying? Do you need my blood? One of my kidneys? A lung? We're the same blood type, so whatever will help you to live, bro, it's yours."

"Thanks, but I'm not sick or dying. I figured since you're an expert in sexual matters, that I'd come to you."

The scrunched brows and downcast mouth relaxed before Zik returned to the bar to make their drinks.

The second Zik handed over the liquor, Zareb downed it in one gulp. The burn of the amber fluid left his voice hoarse.

"More."

"No, thank you. I don't need you passing out here. Everyone would be after me if they found out. Tell me what's going on."

He set the glass on the table. "A young man kissed me. For that millisecond that I let it happen, I could've sworn it was Malika. I know it sounds ridiculous and impossible, but that's what it felt like."

Reality had hit that he was betraying Malika. With not only a guy, but her little brother. What kind of mess was he embroiled in? Guilt and confusion had driven him to shove Sule away.

To his credit, Zik's expression remained neutral. Not a common occurrence.

Zareb spent the next few minutes explaining about Sule and how he'd been reacting to the young man. The mention of the kiss this evening after having made love to Malika released the hinge in Zik's jaw.

"I see. Would you like another drink?"

"No."

Whatever had constricted his ribcage as soon as he'd realized what he'd done with Sule loosened. It felt good to talk. Or maybe it was the liquor.

"How do you feel about Malika?"

Not what he'd expected, but a fair question. "I really like her."

Once again, Zik's mouth dropped open.

"What? I'm capable of emotions."

"I know. It's the admission of it that's got me stunned. Can you go a little deeper? You've known her for what? Three weeks as an adult? What makes you think you *like* her rather than merely being attracted to her?"

"I can't explain how. I just know that I do."

"Not good enough, Reb."

He rubbed damp palms against his thighs.

"She slips into my thoughts when I least expect it, and I allow her to linger, wondering what she's doing and how she is. I ache to be with her. And when we're together, I'm calm and happy. A sense of rightness drapes over me like a blanket while in bed during the cooler months of the year."

He looked at his older brother who wasn't snickering at the outpouring of the sentiments. "The first time I saw her, I was overwhelmed with familiarity."

"You mentioned that you played with her siblings as children. Could she have been in your subconscious?"

"No." He rubbed the centre of his chest. "It's more. I swear, Zik, when we were introduced at the party, I got the sense that my soul danced. It was the most elation I've ever felt. As if everything was right with the world at that moment. Nothing else mattered except for being with her." He sighed. "She's an amazing woman who doesn't back down from me and speaks her intelligent mind. Several hours on the phone chatting, and I don't get bored."

"That's not the Zareb I know. You'll shut down a conversation by walking away within seconds. No excuses given."

"I don't want to do that with Malika. I like hearing what she has to say and sharing with her. She possesses a grit that I appreciate. It fuels me. Once I started getting to know her, I feel as if every decision I've ever made led to meeting her."

"That's deep." Zik wiggled his brows. "Let's talk about the sex with Malika. Details are welcome."

His playboy brother was always sharing about his conquests. Zareb had never seen it as fair to the women he'd slept with.

"Let's leave it at incredible."

He hardened thinking about how perfectly they'd fit together. The movement of her riding him before she'd climaxed, making him come so hard that he'd blacked out.

"What about Sule? What do you feel about him?"

"Stressed," he answered honestly. "He sets me on edge."

Zik snorted. "It's a quality of all teenagers."

"There's something about him that seems off. I can't pinpoint it."

"Do you think about him the same way you do Malika?"

He considered the question. "Unless I'm with him, or planning his workout, I don't think about him at all. And even when we're together, he reminds me so much of Malika that occasionally, I get the warped sense that it's her, especially when he smiles."

"Do you get turned on at the thought of having sex with him?"

Zareb shifted in his seat, uncomfortable with the direction of the conversation. But he wouldn't run.

"I've been thinking about it a lot, even when I really didn't want to. I'm attracted to him." The world didn't implode with his admission. "But I've never wanted to have sex with him. With Malika, it was all I wanted to do. Still is. Being kissed by Sule somehow seemed ... familiar."

"Have you ever had a relationship with a man?"

"No."

Cool and clinical Zik maintained eye contact. "Have you ever wanted to?"

Zareb took a minute to contemplate it. Funny how he was becoming more relaxed about the topic. Other than Sule, he'd never been attracted to another male. If Sule were older, and not Malika's brother, would he want to be with him?

"No."

Zik nodded. "People can be attracted to you when you don't feel the same way about them. And vice versa. That's okay. It's just life screwing with you. I should know. I've been on both ends of that awkward coin."

Zik laughed while Zareb looked at his brother with amazement. There was so much he didn't know about him. He'd make the time to get to know him better. For now, he had a problem to solve. "Back to me, Zik."

"Let's say I have friends who identify as bisexual—"

"Do you think I'm bisexual?"

Zik raised a brow. "Do you?"

His instincts told him no, but then, what was going on with Sule? "I don't know anymore."

"I'm glad to see that you're willing to discuss this with an open mind. Here's the thing though, bisexuality means men and women will appeal to you equally. It all comes down to the individual that you're attracted to, not their gender. Does that make sense?"

The response brought on further confusion. "Kind of. What's going on with Sule, then?"

"I'm not sure. All I can advise is that you be open. Your greatest skill is listening to your gut. If something is off about the boy, then you'll discover it. I've met him, and he seems like a good kid. A bit effeminate, quiet and reserved, but respectful."

The young man could be a mumbling smart ass on occasion.

"Try not to do the Zareb thing by being hard on yourself."

He released a low chuckle. "Unlikely, but I'll try."

"Good."

"Thanks, Zik."

His sibling got to his feet. "What's a big brother for?"

"To use my place as a brothel when it suits him."

Zik let out a robust laugh. "That, too."

CHAPTER TWENTY-TWO

The light breakfast of tea and buttered toast might be coming up at any moment. No matter how hard she tried, Malika had difficulty keeping her nerves from attempting to tangle themselves. Zareb had organized an intense tournament. Competitors from Africa and Europe had arrived to participate.

Her gaze roamed the crowded gym and found him talking to a group of officials. The sexy man had paired a tailored kiss-his-perfect-body midnight blue suit and white shirt with a red paisley tie. She quelled the urge to grab and drag him into an empty room. Those kinds of thoughts would only lead to another debacle of humiliation.

The conversation he'd had with Sule the morning after the impromptu kiss had sent a chill of dread crawling over her scalp as if she had lice. The workout that day had been a nightmare, but she didn't break, grateful that he hadn't decided to throw her out of his gym.

As if he'd used exhausting her as a truth serum, he'd spoken in the most frightening tone she'd ever heard. "What the hell possessed you to kiss me yesterday?"

Too fatigued and mortified to raise her eyes to meet his, she'd shrugged.

"Sule."

She'd jumped to her feet as the roar of her name echoed through the gym, drawing the attention of the early users.

"Do. Not. Play. With. Me." Each word had been severely enunciated.

"I don't know." Her voice had shaken. Only the truth would do at this point. "I like guys."

Her brother wouldn't appreciate this one bit.

"What does that have to do with me?"

"Um ... Well. You're the most attractive man I've ever been around. I made a mistake."

Arms crossed and stance wide, he'd bent at the hips until he was right in her face. "At the cost of hurting your sister? Not wise."

She'd stumbled backwards with her shock. The queen had been right. He really cared about her.

Recovering, she'd frowned. "I realize that, and I'm sorry."

"Are you going to tell your sister, or will I?"

The blinking had become rapid-fire as she'd attempted to figure out what kind of man she'd fallen in love with. Righteous. Disciplined. Sexy. The adjectives had flooded her. The one that had banged around the hardest was magnificent. She'd found a wonderful man to give her heart to.

If only *forgiving* were amongst that list.

"Well, young man?"

"I'll tell her."

"Good."

She'd lowered her gaze to the gym floor.

His heavy hand on his shoulder had stunned her into looking up at him.

"I'm flattered, but I'm into women. Someday, you'll find someone who returns your affections."

"Yes, Your Highness."

It had fascinated her to discover that he had a broader thinking mind than she'd given him credit for. Although, what had she expected? That he'd beat Sule to a bloody pulp? It wasn't his way. Yet, Zareb being tolerant of any sexuality other than hetero impressed her considering the narrow-mindedness of their culture on the topic. Completely frustrating.

Malika snatched herself from the memory of the conversation and fought not to stare at a corporate-looking Zareb.

Focus. You're here to rule this competition, not appreciate gorgeousness at its best.

She returned her attention to the competitors who were warming up like she should be doing.

The competition included a female category that she hadn't expected. The women would fight each other instead of having mixed matches.

Malika would contest in the male category. And win.

***

Every muscle in Zareb's body flexed with the competitive hunger to join the tournament. The clanging of metal and buzzing of the machines indicating a scored point thrilled him.

It always had, and he missed it. He'd made his choice to protect the royal family, and he'd stand by it.

He picked up Sule's épée. The sword was light. Even lighter than it should have been for someone his size.

The young man held out his hand, awaiting his sword, and Zareb gave it over. Sule had made it to the quarter-final round with his impressive skill and speed. No matter how far he proceeded in the competition, Zareb would continue training him. How could he not? He was an exceptional athlete and would get better under his guidance.

The frank talk he'd had with him had been productive. Sule's crush would fade.

Yet, he still questioned his own reaction to him. After talking with Zik, he'd decided that it wasn't necessary to understand. A few things in life could remain a mystery while others, he'd hunt down the answers to until a full discovery was revealed.

He provided Sule one last piece of coaching advice. "You must infight."

Nothing new, but it was imperative that he understand.

The boy's features tightened. With determination or annoyance, Zareb couldn't decipher.

"I've been watching him," he continued. "He's good. Only because he's aggressive, not because he uses the best form or techniques. You have both."

Sule's eyebrows shot up with a slight curve to his lip, looking so much of Malika that a pang of longing cuffed him in the gut. He squashed it, reminding himself that Malika was miles away.

"Don't back down," he said. "If you do, you'll lose. You can't serve two masters. Either you commit to going for the win, or you don't."

Just as in life.

The referee called the competitors to the fencing strip. After showing their respect, Sule and his opponent, Philip, got into the *en garde* position. As soon as the official told them to start, Sule initiated an attack that ended with a lunge that landed his sword on his Philip's hip. The buzz of the score machine stimulated cheering.

Zareb hid his smile behind a hand. Sule certainly knew how to implement coaching instructions. The move had been powerful, but risky because of the chance he'd taken of losing his balance.

Back in position to fight, Sule's opponent wasn't to be taken by surprise again. He went on the offensive right away. Sule retreated with ease, not allowing himself to be hit. With a sudden burst of movement, Sule advanced forward. The speed of both fighters made it difficult to tell which of the two scored the point when the signal went off.

Zareb would place his money on Sule. Turning to the scoreboard, like everyone else, he was correct. Applause erupted. It was still early in the three-minute match—the result could go either way.

Back on the piste, the two warriors faced off again. In a move Zareb had only ever done a few times during competitions, Philip advanced and jumped high, crouching in the air before driving his sword down. Sule didn't stand a chance, although he did attempt to block it when the épée came down on his head.

The crowd had no loyalty. Their cheering rose to near-deafening levels at the perfectly executed manoeuvre.

Sule tipped his head to his adversary.

In the longest, least exciting bout of the match, the next point went to Philip. A tied score. Only fifteen seconds left.

When the fighting continued, the competitors used the advantage they had over the other. Arm extended, Sule brought his rear leg forward and burst through with a classic *flèche* attack to the chest. Concurrently, Philip had counter-attacked, striking Sule on the inside of his elbow. Sule drove past Philip for a few steps with the momentum of his manoeuvre. When the shrill beep rang out, Zareb couldn't tell who had scored the point. It didn't matter when he saw Sule with his mask off, grabbing his sword arm.

Zareb sprinted onto the piste. "What's wrong?"

Sule removed his hand with a wince. There was a tear in the jacket, and a tinge of red stained the white uniform. Was that blood? The medic rushed over and put on gloves before assessing the injury.

He glanced up at Philip to see him scratching his head and scowling as he stared at the broken tip of his sword. Zareb scanned the area. On the floor, not far from Sule, was a small piece of metal, no longer than two inches. He'd bet that it would fit the end of the broken épée. A broken blade wasn't a stupefying occurrence. Someone getting injured from it was.

"Let's get to the treatment room. I need to get you undressed to examine the wound," Dr Keita said while applying pressure to a gauze she'd put on.

When Sule took a step, the silent crowd cheered. He raised his uninjured hand. The walk to the first-aid room seemed to take forever.

Behind closed doors, Sule sat on the examination table.

"Please take off your jacket," Dr Keita said.

Sule attempted to shirk away. "I'm fine, really."

Had the boy taken a blow to the head, too?

"You're bleeding. We need to see the extent of the damage." Zareb remained calm as his heart hammered wild and fast.

The doctor touched Sule's shoulder. "Prince Zareb is right."

Tearless pleading filled the young man's eyes as he turned to the medical personnel.

"I'd prefer you to do it," Sule ground out. "It's probably just a scratch. The prince should leave. He has a lot to take care of, and I don't want to waste his time."

The request had no chance of being granted as Zareb took charge by unzipping and removing Sule's fencing jacket.

"Wait. I ..." Sule swallowed hard as his face scrunched. "I need to tell you something."

The young man held Zareb's wrist with surprising strength when he went to unhook the plastron, the underarm protector used as extra protection just in case of a broken blade. The edge of the sleeve had soaked up blood and was hiding the injury.

He ignored Sule and removed the garment. Dr Keita stepped in to inspect the wound.

"Prince Zareb, I'm—"

"Now is not the time," he said in a commanding tone that nobody dared question. "Let the doctor do her work."

"It's a small cut that will need stitches," the doctor said a moment later. She stood and grabbed a large green case with a white cross on it.

Relieved, Zareb shifted his vision from the wound to Sule's face. He noticed that the T-shirt didn't lie flat against his chest. There was something he wore underneath. He reached out.

Sule pushed his hand away before he could. Not to be deterred, Zareb used his other hand and made contact. The garment was hard.

That could be only one thing.

Like a tsunami wave, understanding crashed. His left foot stepped back in order to keep him balanced, to keep him from stumbling as everything he'd experienced with Sule and Malika during the past six weeks flashed before his eyes.

It all made sense. Hoping he was wrong, he looked into Sule's eyes. "Why do you wear a chest protector?"

Sule flung his gaze to the doctor. "Can we talk about this later?"

Men didn't have to wear the equipment, but it was mandatory for women. Considering that Sule's chest was flat rather than with the bumps of a female chest guard, he held out hope that Sule just preferred using it like a few of his male fencing colleagues had. The intuition he'd ignored for so long blazed.

"No. Answer me now."

"To protect my chest."

His anger rose. "Sule!"

He lowered his gaze and opened his mouth to speak, but closed it.

"Take off the plate."

He snapped his eyes up to his. "Prince Zareb, please."

His stomach sank even further. He already knew what his protégé would say when he pressed. "Then tell me the truth."

"I use it to protect my breasts," he said in a small voice. "I'm Malika."

CHAPTER TWENTY-THREE

Horrified at how the revelation had gone down, Malika would give anything to know what ran through his mind.

Daring to look into his eyes, all she could interpret was fury. Disappointment radiated from him like the stench from hot garbage.

Dr Keita's clearing of the throat did nothing to ease the suffocating tension in the room. "As I mentioned, you're going to need sutures."

"Does he—" Zareb glared at Malika. "—*she* need to go to the hospital?"

The woman stepped back a little bit. "No, I can do the stitching here."

Malika had never had the procedure done, but her older brother had described the injections used to numb the area as worse than obtaining the cut itself. To keep her mind off the incoming torment, with a heavy heart, she watched Zareb stalk across the small room, lean his shoulder against the wall, and cross his legs at the ankles.

His casual appearance didn't deceive. Those flared nostrils and hardened eyes told her everything. Their budding relationship had crashed before it had gotten the chance to lift off the ground.

Swallowing, breathing, even just existing for these few moments became the hardest of her life. She'd had love. He may not have been in love with her, but she'd fallen in a way that had bound her to him. No matter how he felt, she'd always love him. She held out hope that the strength of her affection could keep them together.

Doubtful.

She shut down the pessimist and chose to believe. There was no other option she'd accept. She'd infuriate him even more if she leapt and begged at his feet for forgiveness. That would come later.

"It won't take long, Your Highness," Dr Keita said while preparing. "You can return to the competition if you'd like."

"I'll stay."

The next twenty minutes weren't as bad as her brother had made it seem to be. She tolerated the numbing injection with a sharp inhale through pursed lips.

Distracting herself from Zareb's looming presence across the room, she watched the needle disappear then reappear again on the other side of the wound three times over.

After covering the dressing with one last piece of plaster, the physician arched her back in a stretch. As she cleaned the organized mess she'd made, Malika closed her eyes. How could she initiate the necessary discussion she needed to have with Zareb?

"I'll change your dressing in two days. Keep it dry, which means protecting it with plastic if you decide to shower. The sutures will stay in for ten to fourteen days, depending on how it's healing."

Where would she be when it was time for them to come out? In the palace, or tossed out on her ear and having returned back home?

She had to find a way to make Zareb understand.

After cleaning her hands, the doctor helped her to dress in the clothes Zareb had retrieved from her locker during the procedure. It had been the only time she'd been able to relax. The secret was out, so there was no need to bind her breasts, but she didn't have a bra with her, so she kept the binder on.

The doctor held out a packet of pills. "I'm leaving you some pain medication. You were lucky. If the sword had gone any deeper, you may have severed a tendon."

It could also be said that the freak accident had to be one of the unluckiest things that had ever happened to her. Of course, she'd get stabbed through protective gear with a tournament épée, then expose her true gender to the man she'd fallen in love with. Karma had a nasty way of saying, "*Gotcha!*"

The doctor exchanged words with the prince that Malika couldn't hear.

"Let's go."

The fierce anger in Zareb's voice caused her more anguish than being stabbed.

She swallowed around the heavy lump in her throat and swung her legs over the edge. Light-headedness took over when she stood, so she leaned heavily against the cot.

Her lover made no attempt to assist. A sword piercing her and then getting sewn up hadn't made her cry. His indifference brought on a burn behind her lids. Wrestling her pride to the forefront, she tamped down any sign of weakness.

Applause and shouts greeted her as she stepped into the gym. She raised her left arm and waved as she meandered to the area she'd sat for most of the tournament when she hadn't been competing.

Once seated, her last opponent came up to her and bowed before he squatted so they were closer to eye level.

"I'm sorry for the pain my broken épée has caused you," Philip said with the softy rolled 'r's of a South African accent. "I never would have expected such a thing to happen."

"It's okay. It was a peculiar accident." She held out her bandaged arm. "As you can see, I'm fine."

"I'm glad. Thank you for an energetic match."

Malika wondered if he'd feel the same if he knew he'd fought a female. Males and their egos could never be predicted.

"You, too."

She still had no idea who'd won. They'd both landed solid strikes at nearly the same time. Logic dictated that since she could no longer fight, her adversary would proceed to the next round.

What did any of it matter since the price had been losing both her coach and her man?

Curiosity wouldn't allow her to stay silent. "Who won that last point?"

"I did."

She dipped her head in acknowledgement, allowing good sportsmanship to rule her response. "It was well-earned."

"Thank you." He offered his hand, and they shook. "I'm sure that I will meet you in future competitions. Until then, I will practice defending against infighting."

Malika chuckled.

Her gaze drifted to Zareb. His back was rigid, and she could hear the terse instructions he gave to the coaches and officials while assessing the clipboard of the matches which had occurred during her fix-up.

He turned and caught her staring. Without reaction, he pivoted, giving her his back.

Not even her initially inspired optimism could prevent the depressing harshness that smacked her at realizing that she'd officially lost him.

***

"May I have your attention please?"

Scanning the room from the podium at the front of the gym, Zareb's traitorous gaze kept up its pull to Malika against his will. Having anything to do with the woman who'd made him out to be a huge fool was the last thing he wanted, and yet, he kept glancing in her direction to make sure she was okay.

His skin prickled when Malika's mouth puckered as she shifted positions. Was she in a lot of pain? Maybe she needed something stronger than what had been prescribed. Why should he care?

He'd been an idiot. Even his toddler nephew had greater deductive skills than him to have figured out that Sule and Malika were the same person. He'd known from the beginning that something was off about Sule. His gut had tried to warn him. Why hadn't he dug deeper?

An ear-piercing shriek made the crowd groan. He loosened his grip on the neck of the microphone.

When silence prevailed, he announced the winners for the various styles.

The fourth, third, and second-place winners for the male épée category claimed their places when called. "The first-place champion is Philip Nkosi from South Africa."

The crowd cheered for the man who had beaten Malika by one point at the last second and gone on to win two more matches.

To be fair and honest was the only way he knew. He'd revealed to the other coaches and officials that Sule was a woman. He'd been the one to bring up the question of disqualifying her. They'd read through the competition's by-laws. There was no rule which stated that same genders had to fight each other.

He'd left it up to his officiating team to decide Malika's fate. They'd unanimously agreed to give her the fifth place that she'd earned.

Being a woman didn't downgrade the scores she'd obtained. Instead, it had impressed everyone.

Left with one last certificate to distribute for the participants who didn't place, he tapped the paper, struggling to keep a scowl from his lips.

"Congratulations to Ms. Malika Ahvanti who entered the competition as Sule Ahvanti. We'd like to wish her a speedy recovery."

Malika stood and walked with her head high towards the front. The crowd's murmurs gathered volume before wild applause and shouts of encouragement shook the gym's walls.

The electrical zip in their handshake jarred him. Looking into her eyes was a no-go area, so he gave his attention to the camera as he presented the certificate, wanting the moment to be over so he'd never have to see her again.

The honourable side of him reared up. As much as he hated to admit it, he had to take partial responsibility for her competing with the men.

Yet, understanding the deception didn't eradicate the extreme sense of betrayal of having gone through it.

CHAPTER TWENTY-FOUR

Zareb raised a fist to pound on Zed's apartment door, then thought better of it. It would be a shame to wake his nephew if he was asleep. Not that he'd mind being around the energetic boy, but Rio would bite his head off, and Zed would enjoy watching it happen. He settled on a regular knock.

When the door opened, so did his mouth. "He's a woman."

Zed backed out of the way. "What are you talking about?"

He whipped around from the other side of the room. He wouldn't have to explain if his brother had stayed at the tournament longer than the opening ceremony. "Sule is Malika."

"Still not clear."

Clenching his jaw, he relaxed it only after taking a few rounds of the room. Ever since he'd learned Malika's devious secret a couple of hours ago, he'd been jumpy with the need to express his frustration by smashing his fist into anything that came near him. A foreign experience that he wished to do away with. There would've been a lot less to explain if Zik hadn't been off on one of his grand adventures.

Zik would've witnessed the debacle first-hand as he was the only one who enjoyed fencing almost as much as Zareb did. The rest of his family had left the tournament as soon as the photo ops had been completed.

"I just learned, through a freak accident, that Malika and Sule are one and the same person. She's been pretending to be a male."

He dropped onto the couch and held his drooped head in his hands. "I've been an incompetent imbecile for letting a deceptive snake get so close to me. I knew something was off with Sule, but I couldn't pinpoint it."

He scrubbed his palms down his face. She hadn't even lied about liking men when he'd questioned her male counterpart after kissing him.

Zed's smirk fuelled Zareb's frustration.

"Bro, this has got to be the funniest thing I've ever heard," he said before breaking into an uproarious round of laughter.

Zareb's temper peaked.

His brother wouldn't be so amused if he knew the angst he'd experienced over this sham. He went to the refrigerator and pulled out a juice so that he wouldn't leap forward to throttle his twin. Popping the top, he drained half the bottle while Zed got himself under control.

Zed wiped the tears of mirth from his cheeks as he sighed, indicating the end of his entertained state. "You know our mother had everything to do with this, right?"

"Malika couldn't have gotten in without her support."

Zed snorted. "It was probably Mama's idea. I should've picked it up when she didn't question me when I went to get Malika's contact info. She kept going on and on about how wonderful she thought the young woman was, knowing I'd relay every word. I hate being played."

You're not the only one. Zareb chugged down the rest of the mango-guava drink. "What could she have been thinking?"

"She's pretty vocal about your hard and fast rule of not training women being asinine and needing to be amended. Besides, you know she doesn't need a reason to do anything."

If he wasn't fuming, Zareb would take a moment to appreciate how well his mother had executed her machinations.

"Reb, what's bothering you most?"

"The fact that I've been lied to and deceived isn't enough?"

Zed clicked his tongue as he waggled a finger. "I don't think so. Be honest. You're in love with Malika."

"She's dead to me," he mumbled.

The statement fell miles short of holding the vitriol that it should. As soon as he learned how to eradicate her from his every thought, then it would be true.

"You don't allow any woman close enough so you can even dip your toe in that particular river of emotion."

He glared at his twin. "What's your point?"

"You'll use any excuse to stay out of a relationship."

The quiet in the apartment registered. He berated himself for not noticing it before. A glance at his watch showed the time to be ten. "Where's my nephew and Rio?"

"Visiting her friend. They'll be back soon"

A topic change was just what he needed. "Bachelor for a few hours, then? Must be nice. What were you up to?"

"As I was saying, it's not so much the charade that's upsetting you, but the fact that you've found someone you trust enough to want a commitment with."

Which then gave her the access to shred him emotionally. Trust was overrated. Relationships even more so. The walls were closing in on him, and the air had become stale and hard to draw in. He needed to get out of there.

In a flash, as if anticipating the move, his brother blocked his way when he stood.

"There's nowhere you can go that you can hide from me, so I don't know why you're trying. Consider me your mirror." Zed chuckled at his little joke. "Admit that you want her in a forever kind of way, forgive, and then go after her."

"You know it's not that easy."

"Things are only as difficult as we make them. Do you love her?"

Looking into the steel-grey glinted version of his own eyes, Zareb couldn't lie or hide. "Yes."

"Ha! I could see it coming from a mile away. Now go talk to her to find out her side of the story. If it's legitimate, which I have a feeling it is, then hook up." Zed pointed an index finger. "Believe me, you never want to let the woman you love go."

Zareb recalled the misery Zed had gone through before ending up with his wife and child. "If your situation is anything to go by, then I don't want to ever experience it."

"Does that mean you're going to her?"

He couldn't. Not when thinking about her dishonesty still caused his shoulders to tense. He'd probably end up saying something he'd regret if he met with Malika now. Would the pain ever go away enough for him to not see a lying, scheming, dubious woman? Not the first to have screwed him over.

"I'll think about it."

Which he wouldn't.

***

"How many times do you want me to tell you what happened?" Malika asked her friend.

Shoshana had video-called to inform her about their latest client and had ended up with an earful of the Zareb debacle.

A night of crying had left her voice hoarse and her nasal passages congested. The red, puffy eyes had been a dead giveaway to her misery.

"At least four. My memory is crap, and I need to be able to write some of this down when we get off the phone so I can capture it in full and grand detail if I ever have to write your biography."

Malika snorted.

"Girl, I'm serious. Anyone who gets stabbed with a fake sword needs her own book. By the way, congrats on whooping those guys' asses. You being an Olympic contender will draw in the clients."

"I won't be going anywhere if I don't find a coach. Zareb is out of the question."

"Why? Just because you lied to get him to acknowledge your skill doesn't mean he won't train you."

"Come on, Shoshana. Stop being sarcastic."

"I'm being sincere. If the fact that people lie stopped progress, everyone's resumés would have to go through some intensive scrutiny."

"This is a lot more serious than that."

Her friend grunted.

"Not from where I'm sitting. You have the potential to be the best at what you do. I'm sure he recognizes that and wouldn't be stupid enough to lose the possibility of claiming you." Shoshana waved her hands. "No. Forget I said that. Come back to the US. We'd love to have you. We need even more representation of Black female excellence in the Olympics. Get your ass back here."

For the first time in a couple of days, Malika laughed. "You're too much."

"What did the queen say?"

Yesterday, she'd drudged up the strength to meet Queen Zulekha for lunch in her quarters. The conversation had been both touching and frustrating. Just like the woman.

"He takes after me in more ways than my other children," the queen had said. "We have a lightning-quick temper, but it burns out easily. It's sad." She'd sighed, as if lamenting her inability to sustain a state of rage. "In the end, our initial reactions are quite cathartic." A royal finger had pointed to the ceiling. "Maybe not for the person we explode on."

Didn't she remember that her son had cast out all women from entering his coaching sphere for the past couple of years? He possessed more than a short-fledged temper.

"That's just it. He didn't yell or even chastise me." Malika's shoulders had slumped. "He avoided me."

She'd jumped at Queen Zulekha's unexpected clap.

"That's even better. It means he wasn't truly angry. He'll get over it. Yes, we deceived him, but he'll understand once you explain."

Malika had slapped a hand to her chest and regretted it as pain shuddered from her wound.

"Me?" It had come out as a high-pitched wheeze. "Wouldn't it be better coming from you? It was your idea for me to act like a young man."

"No, darling. I can't get involved. This is between you and Zareb. The resolution of this conflict will set the stage for your future."

"But ... but ..." she had sputtered, not believing what she'd heard. The queen had been intrusive throughout the whole venture, and now, she was willing to back down? Unbelievable.

"I'm sure he's figured out my involvement, so I'll have to smooth his ruffled feathers. If I attempt to advocate on your behalf, he'll fight it." She'd tapped a finger to her chin. "I believe he gets his stubbornness from me, too."

No doubt.

"You mentioned leaving the palace tomorrow. I wish you wouldn't."

"What's the point of staying? The doctor said that I couldn't start training again for a few weeks. Besides, Zareb won't look at me, much less coach me. Not after ..."

Queen Zulekha had sliced into her egg fried yam as if Malika's world wasn't crumbling.

"Have you asked him?"

"Well, no. I presumed that after everything that happened, he'd sack me."

The queen's keen eyes had held hers. "Can I suggest that you talk to my son before slinking away and hiding in your family home?"

Malika had sighed. "I'm afraid."

"Of what?"

She'd bitten her bottom lip to stop it from quivering. "That he never wanted me. Not enough to try to give us a chance after I messed up so badly. His pride was caught up in the situation, so I don't think he'll ever forgive me."

A sob had escaped.

The queen had pushed her seat from the table and come to her.

"Oh, my sweet Malika."

The tenderness of the older woman's embrace had been reminiscent of her mother's, and the dam of emotion had broken.

"That's it, sweetheart, let it all out. You've been strong for much too long. Helping to take care of your family after such a grievous loss. Sacrificing your fencing career, putting your business in jeopardy by moving across the world, and now this."

The tears had cascaded down her face as she'd held onto the queen. The woman who offered her the closest thing to a mother's love.

Replete from crying, she'd felt better. Not back to her normal self, but she could see that running away wouldn't help her get back the man she loved.

"Thank you, Queen Zulekha."

Soft hands had clasped her cheeks. "You are mine. I'm not trying to, and never could replace your mother, but please call me Mama."

Her eyes had watered again. She'd heard Zareb call her that. "Mama."

The queen's throat had bobbed with a heavy swallow. "Good."

Her voice had come out husky, and she'd cleared it as she returned to her seat.

"Can I give you some advice."

Even more comfortable with the older woman, Malika had chuckled. "Can I stop you?"

"You're a quick learner. It will please me to teach you the ways of becoming a princess while you recover from your injury."

Her mouth had dropped open. The queen had reached out to hook a finger against her chin and raise it.

"Lesson number one. Royalty does not gape."

"I don't understand. I'm not a princess. Why would I need to learn to be one?"

The smile had been worthy of a portrait. "Because, my darling, the moment you marry my son, you will be one."

"But ... I ..."

"Mark my words. Zareb will forgive you. It will help if you're always in his domain. I find that I can avoid the temptation of cake when it isn't in the house. Once it's in front of me, it's as good as consumed."

"Am I supposed to be cake?"

The queen had laughed. "No, he doesn't eat sweets. You're going to be what Zareb loves most in the world."

She had raised her brows. "What's that?"

"Someone to protect."

Malika blinked at the screen to find Shoshana waving and calling her name.

"What did you say?" she asked.

"Did the queen tell you that you didn't have a chance?"

"The opposite," she said with a bit of hope. "She told me not to give up on him or my dream."

"The queen sounds like me. She must be amazing!"

"She definitely is. Just like you."

"Aww."

Malika rolled her eyes. "Let's get to work."

Shoshana's orange-glossed lips turned downward. "I'd rather hear about you and Zareb doing the deed. Was it good?"

"I'm not discussing it," she said as she nodded several times with a loopy grin on her face.

Her friend laughed. "I knew it. Nobody gets this upset when the sex is bad. I'm glad you're feeling a little better. Since I can't get the tea, I'll settle for making more money."

"Smart woman."

CHAPTER TWENTY-FIVE

"You called for me, Mama?" Zareb asked in a droll tone resembling his sister Amira's when she was being her respectful type of sassy.

He'd spent the past couple of days after the tournament doing two things: avoiding a confrontation with the domineering, controlling woman who'd raised him, and trying to get over Malika.

He'd discovered that getting Malika off his mind was as futile as tracking an angel. Her essence had tainted everywhere he enjoyed, so how could he forget about her? He'd slept in a room at the palace just so he didn't have to look at his couch, bed, or bathroom and recall how their time together had been the most incredible experience of his life.

"Don't stand at the entrance sulking, love." She patted the couch. "Come in and sit."

When he did as ordered, she tucked a stray loc into his loose ponytail. He'd had little energy to make himself presentable lately. Something that further aggravated him. At least, he hadn't let the situation distract him from work.

"I see that you're irritated," she said in a saccharine tone that grated on his nerves.

He kept his mouth shut. What did she expect him to do? Rage at her? He'd never disrespect her in that manner. Although the passive-aggressive silence hadn't been his natural style, he'd utilized the tactic that would emphasize how deeply he'd been affected by her betrayal.

She triple-clicked her tongue. "I'd expect this avoidance from your siblings, never from you. You must really love Malika to do something so anti-you just to get back at me."

His head started to ache from how hard he clenched his jaw. "She's a liar. And you aided her."

"Yes, I did. But it was for your own good. I'm sure deep down, you knew something was off about the lad. Your intuition wouldn't have failed you."

He'd be damned before admitting to the sparks of attraction he'd experienced when he'd touched Sule or the kiss they'd had because he'd reminded him so much of Malika. "It doesn't change the fact that she isn't who she said she was."

"Did she ever *tell* you she was a male?"

"Now you're insulting my intelligence. She portrayed one, and that's the same as admitting it."

"You have a point." She smoothed her palm over the skirt of her dress. "Her mother, God rest her soul, used to send me videos of her fencing. Her raw talent reminded me so much of you. When she refused to travel far from her family for fear of losing someone close again, I wanted you to work with her."

"You could've just asked me."

"I know you better than you know yourself sometimes. You would've declined the request, even coming from me. You had set your mind to not coaching women, and that was the end of it. Besides, even if you had said yes, you would've never gotten involved with her romantically, and that was more important."

The energy it took to keep his face void of expression could've charged a depleted cell phone battery to full capacity. "Why?"

Her smile crinkled the corners of her eyes. "You two belong together. You're not the only observer in this house."

Oh, how he knew. As children, they couldn't get away with anything because she'd catch them, if not before the act, then right after.

"Zareb, you need to talk to her."

No, he didn't. Even after just two days, his anger and resolve to keep her out of his life had started to fade, replaced by the deep longing to see her again. He feared that an encounter would lead to forgiveness. He couldn't let her back in his life only for her to deceive him again.

"You found the perfect person to coach. You know that she'll be going to the Olympics with or without you. Don't you want to be the one to help get her there?" His mother paused to let the words sink in. "Promise me you'll reach out to her and discuss what happened."

He stood and said nothing. Making such a vow meant he'd have to honour it.

"One." She paused. "Two. Don't make me get to three. Say that you'll see her."

Had he regressed to a four-year-old all of a sudden? He restrained from scuffing the toe of his shoe on the parquet floor. "Fine. But I'll choose when."

That gloating smile of hers deepened his frown.

"Don't wait too long, sugar cane."

He left her apartment with a plan to stay as far away from Malika as time and space would allow.

***

Zareb stopped short at the sight of Malika seated across from his desk when he strode into his office. He'd have to fire every single member of his staff.

"How did you get in here?"

The letter she dangled between her fingers bore his mother's handwriting. "It gives me permission to go wherever I please in the palace."

He held in the groan of frustration at his mother's meddling. The past week had been tough knowing that Malika had remained on the palace grounds. He'd even watched her through the security cameras as she'd walked through the hallways. The creepiness of it wasn't lost on him.

The objective of spying had been to wean himself from wanting her with so much desperation that it made his hands shake. It hadn't worked. His bulging eyes had stayed glued to the monitor as his body ached every time he saw her. All the while, his mind called him a thousand sorts of stupid for staying away from the most amazing woman he'd ever met.

The cold shoulder treatment should've provoked her to leave his country. It would've been a lot easier to get over her without being tempted with her presence every day.

With Malika in the same room, each beat of his heart shouted the word *forgive* as a rush of blood in his ears. Controlling himself from stepping close enough so he could have her firm body melting against him was proving to be an extraordinary challenge.

The room seemed to shrink as he stalked around the periphery to get to his desk. The barrier would help him to control his urges. If only he didn't leap over it to reach her, he'd be fine.

"How may I help you?"

Her back straightened at his cordial politeness.

"I'm here for three reasons. The first is to tell you how sorry I am, Zareb. I didn't mean to hurt you. I don't have a reason that's good enough to have ever deceived you. I could've found another way. A different coach, but ..."

She swallowed hard enough for him to hear.

"I wanted you. A fellow African who defied the odds of being from a small country to make it to the Olympics and won. I wanted to follow in the greatness of your footsteps. To pursue my dreams like I'd promised my mother when she'd been dying. How I went about it was reprehensible. I thought about telling you so many times, but I didn't, and that's not good enough. I can understand if you never forgive me, but please know that I'm sincerely sorry."

The apology had been everything he'd envisioned. Was he ready to forgive? He held her warm brown gaze. He would've done the same thing in her place, especially with his mother's support and prodding. Nothing stopped him when he set a goal.

He'd already forgiven her. Pride had kept him from admitting it. It might take longer for him to forget, but he'd work on it.

No need to let her off the hook that easily, though. "What were the other two things you wanted?"

Her frown tugged at his heart. He held resolute.

"Um. Well. I need your assistance," she said in a low voice.

"With what?"

She took in a deep breath and straightened her spine.

"Thank you for giving my father and older sister clearance to visit me for a few days last week. It was wonderful having them around." She dipped her head to the side. "I wish you could've met them."

He'd known their every movement but had refused to bring himself to engage. Even by his standards, he'd been rude.

"I was busy."

She let the falsehood dangle in the silence of her pause.

"After the competition, my father was of two minds. He was prouder than a peacock that I'd made it so far into it while competing against men who hadn't held back because I was a woman. He was also horrified that I'd gotten stabbed even though I explained that the risk of it happening again was almost impossible. He wasn't having it."

Caught on the expressiveness of her face as she'd spoken, it took effort to understand the meaning behind her words.

"Your father wants you to return home and give up on fencing," he surmised.

Understanding the risk of the sport from the inside, Zareb knew that the chances of such a thing having happened in the first place was statistically ridiculous. Yet, witnessing her pain had caused his own agony to flare, and now, all he wanted was for her to be safe.

Her natural talent exceeded anyone he'd trained. As much as a tiny selfish part of him wanted her to drop the sport, he sought the best for her, which would be to continue competing.

It had taken his temper cooling down to come to the decision that he'd be the one to make it happen. The Olympics would see Malika Ahvanti stand on the upper-most podium holding a gold medal and bouquet of flowers as she waved with her face glowing in joy.

She angled her upper body forward. "On the contrary. My father realized what I and my mother had been trying to get him to understand for years. That I have a chance at being the best."

Her red-glossed lips rose into a broad grin, stirring up the longing to have been the one to have caused it.

"Not only did my fabulous father give his blessing, he also provided me with an unlimited budget to buy the best gear I could find. And since I no longer have a trainer here ..." She glanced up at him through lashes that lacked the filler that she'd worn to deceive him when he'd met her as Malika. "He insisted that I go back to my former trainer in the US."

CHAPTER TWENTY-SIX

Malika clasped her trembling hands together. He hadn't responded to her apology, and it had devastated her.

She wouldn't give up. She'd rather have her pride mopped all over the floor than to be without Zareb. She added to the plan she and the queen had come up with. After the last stage, she'd beg him to take her back. On her knees if she had to. She was desperate to make him see how in sync they'd been. And how great they'd be once they cleared the nastiness of her behaviour.

Did she deserve him?

Yes. She was a human who'd made a mistake. He had to realize that. She wouldn't let herself think about the alternative if he didn't.

This was the one chance she had to win him back, so she'd better make it good.

"I'm still adamantly against being too far away from my family, so I've been doing some research into coaches in Africa and Europe."

Zareb responded with a narrow-eyed glower. She was sure that was on the gigantic list of things royals weren't supposed to do while in public. Her training with the queen had been overwhelming, but fruitful.

She removed a handwritten sheet of paper from the envelope.

"I was wondering if you could get me in contact with any of these coaches." Rather than give him the list, she read off the first name. "Michael Lufton is my first choice."

Zareb's nostrils flared as his upper lip curled into a snarl. "No."

"But he's one of the best." Zareb had beaten him to earn the bronze medal in the 2016 Olympics. Knowing that he detested the man, Queen Zulekha had insisted that he be on the list. "London is only six hours by direct flight, so it would be easy to get back and forth when I need to. Michael has an amazing work ethic and a fencing programme that's highly rated."

"He's a racist. No matter how covert he tries to be about it, it always shines through. So no, you will not train with him."

The pen scraped the paper as she crossed Michael off. "How about Albert Flesch from South Africa? He has an impressive record of training women to contend in the Olympics."

Zareb shook his head in a slow, deliberate motion. This time, those luscious lips tilted down into a frown. "He's never won a medal, and none of the people he's coached has ever placed. He's not the one to train you."

She clamped her mouth to keep from reminding Zareb that he had yet to coach anyone who'd ended up qualifying for the Olympics. "Then how about—"

In a blink, he'd leaned over his desk and yanked the paper from her hand. He assessed it with pen in hand, striking out each name one by one with a valid reason.

Her mouth went dry as he stood, rounded the wooden barrier, and sat in the seat next to her.

She'd missed those focused, penetrating dark eyes that let her know she was the only one in his sights.

"Stay and train with me."

She placed a hand to her chest to prevent her franticly beating heart from bursting out. "But you don't work with women."

"I was wrong to establish that rule. I shouldn't have let the actions of those few blind me to the potential of others."

To be coached by him was one thing, but she wanted more. Him. Would he be able to let go of his anger? To truly forgive her when she was having difficulty doing so herself?

"Why would you want to be around someone you hate with such vehemence?"

"I don't hate you."

She'd be floating to the ceiling any moment now, but things weren't settled. Time to grovel. "Zareb, I really am sorry that I lied to you. If I had to do it over again, I'd have told you earlier."

He considered her for several seconds. "So, you would've done it anyway?"

"Would you have lifted your ban if I'd come to you as Malika asking if you'd train me without proving myself?"

"No."

"If I knew I'd fall in love with you and hurt you with my betrayal, then ..." She reached out and placed a hand against his upper arm. "I would've taken the chance and been upfront. The relationship we'd started building means more than being a fencing champion."

He grasped her hand and leapt to his feet, bringing her with him. When their bodies collided, she grabbed his shoulders.

"You love me."

The wonder in his voice mesmerized her as much as the adoration in his eyes.

"Yes. Do you forgive me? Say that you'll give us another chance. Please."

"I forgive you."

His husky voice sent warmth bursting in her chest.

When he swooped down, wrapping his arms around her, pulling her close, she could've touched the stars.

His mouth crushed hers, and she responded with the desperation she'd felt over the past week. He gentled the kisses with soft nips. The teasing was too much. When she licked his top lip, his groan vibrated through her just before he deepened the kiss.

She let him know with every caress of her tongue just how much she'd missed him. She relinquished the trauma of having lost him. He was hers, and she intended to keep it that way.

The kiss hadn't lasted long enough before he ended it with a peck. Resting his forehead against hers, eyes opened as if not wanting their reconciliation to have been a dream, their rapid breaths mingled.

"What was the third thing you came to me for?"

She squeezed his shoulders. "To tell you that I love you."

He lifted and swung her around. "Will you train with me and bring the gold to Bagumi?"

She started to back away in disappointment, only to be caged in his arms. "Is that all you want from me, Zareb?"

"That. To get to know you." He bent at the knees so they were eye-to-eye. "And to show you how much I love you."

When she placed her hands on his chest, his rapid heartbeat belied his calm. "Then yes, I'll allow you to lead me to the Olympics."

His uncharacteristic guffaw startled her before she added her own laughter in response.

"I knew it the moment I saw you step out from behind the potted plant at my father's party that you'd be someone special in my life. Maybe before then, when I witnessed you talking to yourself. I presumed it was a pep talk because as soon as you stopped, you squared your shoulders and headed my way."

Mortified, she covered her face. "I didn't know anyone could see me."

He gripped her wrists and kissed the palm of each hand. "I did, and I'm glad because that night, I saw your strength. Instead of leaving, you faced a challenge head-on. To be honest, it's good that I got to work with Sule. I was able to push *him* harder than I would have any woman. It taught me a major lesson."

"You almost killed me."

"I propelled you to be more than even you thought you could be. I may have brought on the pain, but you persevered and made me proud."

He held her close, cuddling as if he'd never let go.

If she had her way, he never would.

EPILOGUE

Malika's legs burned as she pushed her sprint into a longer stride. Beating Zareb in anything physical would probably be her forever goal, but she'd never stop trying.

"No fair." She panted as she came to a jogging stop from the race he'd challenged her to. "You're wearing trousers." The grass tickled her toes. "And shoes."

His gaze travelled down the length of the legs she'd bared when she'd hitched up her dress to meet his challenge. Three months together, and she still got butterflies when he gave her that look. The one that would have her tucked into a dark corner with whatever camera that should be watching them switched off.

She backed away as her core heated. "Not now, my prince. We have a party to attend."

The predator in him advanced. "It can wait. You said you wanted to release some stress. There's no better way than for us to—"

She placed her fingers against his persuasive mouth. It wouldn't take much to have her hands and chest pressed against a wall as he filled her from behind.

No. They couldn't. The break from the party had been for him, but she'd keep that secret. Her fiancé hated gatherings. If it had been a manhunt, he would've been floating with reserved joy.

She'd already competed and placed in two international competitions, gaining in rank. Only a natural disaster would stop her from qualifying for the Olympics. When she made it, no matter who she faced off with, she'd win. All thanks to her fantastic coach.

"The engagement party is for us," she reminded him. "It would be rude to skip out on it."

His firm lips nuzzled her neck, stoking the always-present need for him.

She pulled out the big guns. "Your mother says being rude is not a royal activity that we engage in."

His breath tickled her ear. "Anyone who has ever met me knows that there are two rules that I live by."

She clutched onto him as her knees melted at the seduction in his voice. "Protect and serve?"

"No, my princess. Live and love. You make it easy to do both."

She let out a yelp as he swooped her into his arms and carried her farther away from the celebration.

"My shoes."

He didn't glance back in the direction she'd pointed. "We'll get them when we return."

Giving in, she found his nipple through the dress shirt and teased it with the tip of her finger.

"Keep it up, and I'll take you right here in the grass."

Since Zareb had started it, she scraped the skin of his neck with her teeth and soothed the area with circular motions of her tongue. "You wouldn't dare."

When her legs gave way to gravity as he let them go, she clung to his shoulders in a fit of giggles.

"Okay, I'll stop. Everyone knows we're in love. No need to tarnish my reputation as an Olympic hopeful by showing them, too."

He resumed their unorthodox walk.

Malika caressed a hand through the strands of his locs.

"Besides—" she raised herself up so she could whisper in his ear. "Just like everything else we do, I'm sure I'd get addicted to it."

That's when he started running.

Life was never boring with her coach, lover, fiancé, and protector. She wouldn't have it any other way.

THE END

Thank you for reading *The Resolute Prince by Nana Prah*, Royal House of Saene Book 5. Please leave a review on the site of purchase.

ABOUT THE AUTHOR

Nana Prah first discovered romance in a book from her eighth-grade summer reading list and has been obsessed with it ever since. Her fascination with love inspired her to write in her favorite genre where happily-ever-after is the rule.

She is a published author of contemporary, multicultural romances. Her books are sweet with a touch of spice. When she's not writing she's reading, over-indulging in chocolate, and enjoying life with friends and family.

Connect with Nana
Twitter: https://twitter.com/NanaPrah
Facebook: http://www.facebook.com/NanaPrah.Author
Instagram: https://www.instagram.com/nanaprahauthor

Keep reading for an excerpt from *The Tainted Prince by Kiru Taye*, Royal House of Saene Book 6.

EXCERPT—The Tainted Prince by Kiru Taye

The moment Danai placed the wine glass aside and shifted to rise from the settee, Zawadi stopped caring about rules and protocols.

He tilted his head and raised his hand, cupping her cheek. It was the first time he'd touched her intentionally.

Her skin was smooth milk chocolate. Her breath hitched, seemingly from shock by his action. Her lips parted slightly as if an invitation to kiss her.

The big moment didn't pass him by—the seriousness and consequences of his actions, not just on his life but on the kingdom.

He, who had never deviated from the plan set about when he was born, was about to take a massive detour.

He hesitated, teetering over the edge of an invisible cliff. This oasis was far removed from the rest of the world. Yet, others would feel the impact of his deeds.

After the attempt on his life, he'd escaped to this desert palace, where he was surrounded by vaults of ancient scrolls and shelves of books. He'd come to immerse himself in his favourite pastime—studying and preserving his country's history and culture.

Yet, he'd discovered something else. A yearning so intense, so overwhelming, he was coming undone at the seams.

Danai, on her part, stayed composed. Aside from the steady pulse at the base of her throat, she didn't show any anxiety or annoyance. Instead, her brown eyes seemed to watch him without judgement, which strengthened his resolve.

She understood the risk he was about to take, had never pressured him into doing anything about the spark that existed between them from the first time they'd met. The time they'd spent together, her always by his side—the conversations they'd had. Slowly, over time, without knowing it, he'd become emotionally attached to her.

Then she'd laid her cards on the table, told him she cared about him. She'd seen his vulnerability, his fears, and hadn't been repulsed. Hadn't thought less of him.

Now she waited, perhaps wondering if he would take this to the next level and kiss her.

EXCERPT—Note Worthy by Dhasi Mwale

Wezi rubbed the back of his neck and parted his lips into that Wezi-specific half- enchanting, half-nervous grin.

It took a minute longer than she was comfortable with, but Katenekwa regained her cognitive functions and spoke. "Gwen, can you give us a minute?"

Gwen's face registered understanding, and she slipped out the door.

Whatever Gwen assumed she'd understood about Katenekwa's request couldn't be right.

Wezi was, simply put, an undefined complexity in Katenekwa's life. He didn't qualify as an ex because they'd never dated. Instead, he'd been one of her closest friends. Almost family. He'd filled whatever role her life needed, but never the part of a lover. What they did was flirt. Yet, she felt him deep within her in a way that often disqualified the pretentious role of friend.

Wezi stood, closed the space between them with two strides, and gathered her in his arms. She stiffened, then melted, but before she could enjoy his warmth, he pulled away.

And so, they stood facing each other in silence and awe till he spoke. "You look amazing, Kitty."

Wezi, always generous with compliments.

Katenekwa wrapped her tired arms across her chest. An ineffective move with her 38Ds. She fought the urge to drop her arms to her sides, lest he thought she was uncomfortable.

Of course, she was, but he didn't have to know that. For all he knew, his presence here meant nothing. Made her feel nothing. And oh, how she wished it was so.

"You don't look bad yourself," she said and bid her racing heart to still.

Wezi never looked bad. He was attractive without needing to try. Athletic build, extra dark roast coffee skin, face chiselled as if by a sculptor. His effortless beauty sometimes made her feel inadequate about her own looks.

Her pear-shaped figure was at the wrong end of the BMI chart, and she was short, with skin that burned in the sun even though she wasn't light skinned. Oval face, small nose.

In her own right, she was attractive but next to Wezi? Even when he came straight out of bed—drowsy, crusted eyelids, bed-head Afro—Wezi was a looker.

"You cut your hair!" she said with a gasp.

He ran a hand over his short fade. "Yeah. My agent thought I'd book more jobs."

Katenekwa went around the table and collapsed into the chair. "I take it the modelling is going well."

"It's all right. It was weird at first."

Not as weird as it had been for her to come to work one morning and find Wezi's image everywhere. It had been Lillian's idea to use him on the festival's promotional posters. Pretty people grab people's attention.

Katenekwa's longing gaze swept over Wezi. *Ain't that the truth*, she thought. She pulled her attention away from him and chose a spot on the wall behind him to focus on. "So, I saw your name on the program for the festival."

His head bobbed in a partial nod. "Yeah. They called me way back when. I heard you're planning it.

Congrats." He leaned against the wall and crossed his legs at the ankle.

"K pulled a few strings before he...." Her sanity strained at the memory, and she choked. She willed the unpleasantness away. "So, you waited all day? You could have called."

He flashed his teeth. "I thought I'd surprise you, and I wasn't sure you'd want to see me."

Her gaze left the wall for a second. Wanting to see him had never been the issue. It was what she'd do once she saw him that was a problem. "Of course, I'd want to see you."

"That's cool then because I need your help."

"Yeah?"

"Remember when you told me I exemplify the 'starving' in 'starving artist'?"

"I remember saying something like that, yes."

"Well, that hasn't changed all that much. I need a place to stay this week, just until after the show. I won't take much, I swear. I just can't afford a motel room right now."

Wezi went on to explain how he'd be an invisible guest. Sure. Because she could be under the same roof with him and not see him, hear him, or smell him. She'd know. Her body would know. Her heart would know. And thus, it thumped wildly, singing tales of woe. But God, he was so cute. She leaned into her hands and followed the rhythm of his pacing while he explained himself.

He came to a stop in front of her. "What?"

"You do this over-talking thing when you're nervous. It's adorable," she said.

He tucked in his lower lip into what might have been a pout had not the corner of his mouth turned up. "I'm a man. You can't use that word to describe me."

"So adorable!" she said in a mock whisper.

She could refuse. However, that option would require her to confront and verbalize all the pain he'd caused her, and frankly, now was not an appropriate time to go digging in the past. Besides, it was just a few days, and then he'd disappear into the night as only he knew how.

"Okay. You can stay with me. But you know I live in a one-bedroom, right? You'll get the sofa."

"I've slept on worse. Thank you."

"Don't mention it. We're family."

The light in his eyes went out.

EXCERPT—Betting on Love by Kani Sey

Seconds later, Aminata returned followed by a tall, light-skinned young man clad in a starched white shirt and black cotton trousers.

The smile froze on Binta's face when she saw who it was, her body stiffening in shock. Unbidden, his name fell from her lips.

"Bass."

His facial expression transformed from genuine surprise into cool indifference.

"I guess it was too much to hope that our paths will never cross again," he muttered low, seemingly for her ears only.

"Do you know each other?" Aminata asked, looking from one to the other.

Bass nodded. "We were friends, once upon a time."

"Then I'll leave you two to get reacquainted," she said and left the office, closing the door behind her.

"Please have a seat," Binta said.

He pulled out a chair and sat opposite her. His gaze was still fixed on her, unmoving, unwavering, as if like her, he wanted to wake up and discover that this was only a nightmare.

"So, you're a manager," he murmured with the ghost of a smile. "You're really doing well."

Binta felt like a lab specimen trapped under a microscope with the intensity of his stare. She nervously brushed away the escaped tendrils of hair from her face, willing her hands to stop trembling.

He was absolutely the last person she expected to just walk into her office.

Yet, there he was, looking hauntingly familiar and strange all at once.

He appeared as uncomfortable as she was.

She needed to get herself together and make sure he didn't bolt.

It had only been three months since she began working in this bank. Driving clients away wasn't a practice she should engender if she wanted to keep her job.

She fortified herself with this thought and said in her most charming voice. "So, what can we do for you, Bass?"

OTHER BOOKS BY LOVE AFRICA PRESS

Love and Hiplife by Nana Prah

Note Worthy by Dhasi Mwale

Forever and a Day by O.L. Obonna

Saving Her Guard by Kiru Taye

CONNECT WITH US

Facebook.com/LoveAfricaPress

Twitter.com/LoveAfricaPress

Instagram.com/LoveAfricaPress

www.loveafricapress.com

CPSIA information can be obtained
at www.ICGtesting.com
Printed in the USA
LVHW090236310721
694160LV00016B/1477